The Lazarus Syndrome

WHY CAN'T I DIE

A Collection of Resuscitations,
Revivals, NDEs & OBEs Featuring:
A Memoir, Including the Vietnam War

JAIME REYES

ISBN 978-1-966540-32-8 (softcover)
ISBN 978-1-966540-33-5 (ebook)

This book is a work of fiction. Names, characters, places, and incidents are the product of the author's imagination or are used fictitiously. Any resemblance to actual locales, events, or persons, living or dead, is purely coincidental.

Printed in the United States of America.

The Lazarus Syndrome

WHY CAN'T I DIE

A Collection of Resuscitations,
Revivals, NDEs & OBEs Featuring:
A Memoir, Including the Vietnam War

JAIME REYES

Also by Jaime Reyes

En el Principio (Spanish Version)
Short Stories:
"The Shining City by the Sea"
"Lazarus Effect"

Memoirs:
First Night
Guest Columnist:
We Complain (English)
Nos Quejamos (Spanish)

Blogs:
Opciones Para el Futuro de Puerto Rico (Spanish)
Options for the Future of Puerto Rico (English)
Legalization of Marijuana

Dedicated to my Son, Grandchildren and Great-Grandchildren
—Not necessarily in order of preference.

Anthony Sr.	Emily
Anthony Jr.	Jasmine
Edward	Lesley
Julian	Natasha
Jeramiah	Nina
Jaaziah	Lyla
Ronin Jaime	Ameenah
Idris	Leah
Leonardo	Ivy

Table *of* Contents

P A R T E 2

Introduction

"I do not fear death. I had been dead for billions and billions of years before I was born, and had not suffered the slightest inconvenience from it."—Mark Twain

My name is Jaime, the "J" as in Jose or Juan, not as in John. I published my first book in 2018 *"In the Beginning – The Early Days of Religious Beliefs."* My publisher has been urging me for a second book, but they requested a sequel to the first. I was not ready for that. They then suggested a memoir or an autobiography. I told them that I was not yet famous, nor had I accomplished anything worthy of note.

The publisher reminded me that I had mentioned a future book about the Lazarus Syndrome. They didn't really know what that meant but after I explained, they suggested I proceed.

For those that have never heard of the Lazarus Syndrome or the Lazarus Effect, it is a medical event, a quite unusual one but a very real occurrence. It is named after the Biblical Lazurus whom Jesus raised from the dead after four days in the grave. (See Footnotes)

The term describes people who suffer a traumatic event, from a still birth to injury, heart attack or stroke and are officially declared dead by a medical professional but experience a spontaneous resuscitation, minutes, hours, or even days after being pronounced. Some revive quickly but others may take a little longer, even after being placed in a body bag and taken to the morgue. There have been a few who surprised the medical examiner when the first autopsy incision is started. Others have been known to revive in a casket during a wake.

The least fortunate come back to life after burial, but not for long.

This event was more prevalent in years past when doctors were quick to declare death when the heart stopped. These days, brain dead is more accurate, but even that has fooled a few MDs.

I chose the subject because I found it interesting but even more so, because I am a Lazarus Syndrome survivor with the added bonus, that while most of the people cited have done it once or twice, I've toyed with the effect numerous times. It seems that I die easily but don't stay that way.

For the record, this has nothing to do with miracles, religious beliefs, or any sort of divine intervention. Even though a great number of unexplained revivals do thank the heavens for coming back to life, I am a non-believer of any of those supernatural interventions. I prefer to depend on two or more skilled medica/surgical hands working to save me than depending on a thousand pair of hands clasped in prayer pleading for heavenly assistance.

While I do respect those who prefer to thank the powers they choose to believe in, I will also give credit to the medical professionals who use their skill to save lives and bring back some that temporarily slip away.

I've cited numerous examples of those who've returned after beginning the journey to the great beyond, whatever, or wherever that is. At first, I did not include those who claim to have experienced NDEs and claim they were beckoned by a bright light or long-gone relatives, friends, or acquaintances. Very few of those in this book, including myself, saw a light or were greeted by a welcoming party. Nor were any warned to "go back, it is not your time." I found far too many examples of Near-Death Experiences (NDEs) and Out of Body Events (OBEs), to exclude them altogether. Those two experiences deserve attention and at least an attempt at explanation.

 Personally, I experienced nothing, no pain, no sorrow, no worries. It verifies what I've heard during debates between religious and non-religious opponents: Question – "So what do you think there is after death?" Answer- "The same thing there was before birth – Nothing!"

Still, common sense tells me that nobody knows for sure what follows life no matter if that life was great, miserable, well accomplished, filled with disappointment, saintly or devilish. No one has ever come back to detail the hereafter. Some of us have been yanked back from an incomplete occurrence, and therefore have no definitive experience to offer a valid and reasonable explanation or description of what follows.

There is only one of two possible outcomes depending on whether one is a believer or a denier of an afterlife. The deniers will know only if they are wrong. And the believers will only know if they are right, even if the end result is not what they expected or hoped for.

Since my publisher requested I include a memoir, I've added situations that others may consider interesting or even valuable. For those contemplating a college degree, I offer methods to shorten the time required to obtain a four-year degree.

I completed my Bachelor of Science degree in twenty-three months instead of the usual four years, utilizing accredited and legitimate ways of accumulating college credits in a matter of hours instead of boring and costly weeks in class. Many people unknowingly already have valuable credits available just for the asking, and a small fee.

To add variety and a break from stories that may be a bit morbid, In Part TWO I included periods of my life that may satisfy those interested in military service, specifically – my tour in Vietnam, business accomplishments and Law Enforcement activity. There are also short tales detailing situations that were perilous or potentially life threatening that I inexplicably survived with little or no damage. Those events appear under "Close Calls."

Some areas discuss the varied ideas covering the several possibilities of an afterlife even if there is no certified evidence to prove the validity of any of them. Still, the beliefs are firmly held and no amount of discussion to the contrary will dislodge that ideology or mindset.

On occasion I wonder how disappointed some believers will be if their particular sect turns out to be the wrong choice after devoting a lifetime to following the one belief system they chose to follow at an earlier age.

I will leave that conundrum to a future book. This writing explores an event that is not as rare as originally believed and that many have or will experience, especially now that medical science is far more advanced than it was just a few years ago.

Later on, I will examine newer research and developments in the study of Near-Death Experiences (NDEs), and Out-of-Body Experiences (OBEs).

A few pages will cover scientific research into attempts to discover what happens to consciousness or the soul after one is officially declared dead: does it continue a presence, does it hang around, dissipate into nothingness, or does it go anywhere? Believe it or not, there are doctors, philosophers, scientists, and other professionals attempting to discover scientific evidence to either bolster or debunk faith based only opinions on the existence and/or necessity of the soul.

There are others attempting to artificially perpetuate the thoughts and memories of the deceased by uploading them into computer-like devices, including androids, and robots. I may also include some words on cryonics or preservation of human bodies or brains with the hope of someday reviving the frozen person or brain. This process, whether it is potentially feasible or not, for now, is reserved only for the super-rich. Renting a cryogenic container indefinitely can be extremely expensive.

The Lazarus Effect

"People fear death even more than pain. It's strange that they fear death. Life hurts a lot more than death. At the point of death, the pain is over. Yeah, I guess it is a friend.
—Jim Morrison

First, I need to explain what the Lazarus effect is. It is medically known by various names: The Lazarus Syndrome, Lazarus Effect, Lazarus Phenomenon, Lazarus Heart, Autoresuscitation, Autoresuscitation after failed CPR, or **D**elayed **R**eturn of **S**pontaneous **C**irculation after CPR attempts have failed. The usual acronym is **SROC** – **S**pontaneous **R**eturn **of** Circulation. *Gordon L, Pasquier M, Brugger H and Paal P. Autoresuscitation (Lazarus phenomenon) after termination of cardiopulmonary resuscitation – a scoping review. Scandinavian Journal of Trauma, Resuscitation and Emergency Medicine, 2020. 28(14).*

In simpler terms, it is coming back to life after it appears the patient has died especially after being officially declared dead, by a medical professional.

Of course, the name derives from the biblical character, Lazarus who was resuscitated after several days in the tomb.

This is not a new medical condition. In the 17th and 18th centuries, and earlier, some people, especially those of means, were terrified of being buried alive. As a safeguard in case they "woke up" interred in a coffin, they arranged to have a bell mounted outside the grave with the ringer attached to a rope that extended into the coffin. The bell connected to the coffins may have given rise to the terms "dead ringer" or "saved by the bell." - Alexa

I could find no verification that this "safety" coffin method saved anyone from dying as a result of premature burial.

Lazarus Effect
How and Why

"If you don't know how to die, don't worry; Nature will tell you what to do on the spot, fully and adequately. She will do this job perfectly for you; don't bother your head about it."
—Montaigne

The exact cause of the Lazarus syndrome is unknown but there are some theories behind various cases:

Air trapping. Rapid ventilation rates lead to lung hyperinflation and air trapping, which decreases venous return (blood flow return to the heart). This is believed to be more common in those with pre-existing airway disease. Once ventilation is stopped, blood return may be restored, leading to spontaneous circulation.

Drug delay. Drugs injected through a peripheral line may not be able to reach the heart because of high intrathoracic (pressure in the thorax) pressure that occurs with positive pressure ventilation. Once PPV is stopped, intrathoracic pressure decreases, which could allow the drugs to reach the heart. Additionally, there could be a delay in drug effect in a severely acidotic (excess acid in bloodstream) patient.

One or more of the four following possible causes may have played a part in my 2017 incident.

Spontaneous plaque dislodgement. The plaque in the coronary artery may come loose spontaneously after CPR is stopped, leading to restored circulation.

Myocardial stunning. Heart may dysfunction after myocardial ischemia and can last several hours before normal heart function returns.

Transient asystole. Transient asystole can happen after defibrillation, which is why it's important to continue resuscitation after defibrillation. Note: Asystole is when the heart's electrical system fails, and the heart stops pumping. Also referred to as "flat-line" or "flat-lining" because the heart's electrical function displays as a flat line on an EKG. This causes death in minutes without CPR or other treatment.

https://my.clevelandclinic.org/health/symptoms/22920-asystole

Untreated reversible causes. Failure to treat unsuspected reversible causes of cardiac arrest such as acidosis or hyperkalemia (High levels of Potassium), could resolve, leading to restored circulation.

https://www.ems1.com/medical-treatment/articles/rosc-after-death-the-lazarus-syndrome-WfDfxqI9As8diGUq/
-Marianne Myers BS 8/31/2020

Officially Declared Dead

"Fear of death is ridiculous, because as long as you are not dead you are alive, and when you are dead there is nothing more to worry about!" —*Paramahansa Yogananda*

The first case to be discussed is my own initial introduction to overcoming death; as the sub-title, *Why Can't I Die*, suggests, the first of many. Forgive my slightly egocentric choice, but it is the story that has accompanied me all my life and the one I know best. I will have other case histories to describe. Some will be similar to my experience while others will be considered more unbelievable and for some readers, they will be regarded as more miraculous.

My life began in 1945, but not precisely at birth. This chapter of my life does not all come from memory. I do not remember any of the episodes as an infant, except one when I was about five years old. The earlier events were relayed to me by my parents and other family members. My story has become a family legend.

I was a large baby, 11 pounds, and my mother was small and thin, weighing only about 90 pounds, which led to great difficulty for both of us. I got stuck on the way out, unable to breathe and ended up as a "blue baby." When the midwife finally managed to pull me out, she told my mother, *"El Bebe esta muerto"* ("The baby is dead"). She tossed aside the lump of inert flesh and proceeded to take care of my mother who was bleeding excessively.

Due to the unexpected difficulties, a doctor had been summoned to assist early in the process. He arrived at about the same time I did and verified that I was indeed not breathing and had no pulse. My mother kept staring at me through tearful eyes and saw one of my pinky fingers twitch. She screamed, *"Esta vivo!, está vivo."* (¡*"He's alive! he's alive!"*). The physician and midwife began using antiquated CPR practices and eventually restored my normal breathing. One of the methods used was blowing cigar smoke in my face.

The troublesome birth may have led to years of health problems highlighted by severe seizures which made me flop around like a fish out of water.

Several times, during or after some of the most pitiless seizures, I stopped breathing. My father would then run a mile or so to the hospital with me in his

arms only to hear the emergency room doctors or clinicians say, "*Es muy tarde, esta muerto, llevatelo.*" ("It is too late, he's dead, take him back home.")

He, of course, would tell them that I had done this before and all he wanted was a little help or a way to stop the events from repeating or killing me permanently. Only the very severe seizures would interfere with my breathing, but still, the doctors offered no cause or solution. There is no record of the number of events that ended in temporary death. My parents did not keep a diary or a log documenting every event. The hospital kept no records either since I was never an admitted patient. Every time my father brought me in, the doctors told him it was too late, that I was already dead. Perhaps I was better off that they did not attempt untested methods of resuscitation or use primitive tools to diagnose my problem. All they could have done was assume or guess at the causes and even worse how to treat neonatal patients. I have no way of knowing or investigating what sort of training, education or experience the medical people who dealt with me back then may have had, but my current opinion is, that in today's medical environment, they would not be qualified to scrub bed pans.

I often wonder why my parents bothered consulting doctors since they had no idea of the cause or how to treat me. Nor did they have a clue as to how I managed to resuscitate every time.

Since doctors had no diagnosis, they chose to give my mother a fatalistic prognosis. They told her that eventually, I would not resuscitate and in their opinion, not likely to reach age seven. I've always wondered how or why they chose seven years instead of five, six, or eight.

Because of that ominous prediction, and her very strict Catholic upbringing, she opted to recruit the Church and lean on her religious indoctrination and firmly held beliefs. to take a hand in my salvation.

Catholics, and other Christian sects, in drastic situations, ritualistically and, in my opinion, without logic select a saint or virgin from their pantheon of idols and vow to perform some sort of penance or sacrifice so that their prayers are answered. My dear mother selected the Virgin of Monserrate, whom people of her town had chosen as their patron saint. The legend was that she had appeared miraculously and stopped a charging bull from goring a man. By the way, the bull reportedly dropped to its knees in reverence to the apparition. An altar was erected high on a hill near the site of her glorious intervention. Said hill would create an arduous effort for me some years later.

My mother's vow was to let her hair growand wear a monk›s habit for seven years in the hope that divine powers would heal me or keep me from dying repeatedly. Unfortunately, she included me in the vow even though I was an infant and had no say or opinion in the matter. Therefore, my hair would not be cut either and I was dressed in a similar monk's habit (actually, a brown sack dress tied at the waist with atasseled rope.)

The years passed, my hair grew long and was braided into pigtails. Though seizures became less frequent, my many restorations became family legend of the boy that would not die, or at least, did not stay dead. I continued to experience seizures but not all were severe enough to stop my breathing. My mother believed that the virgin had heard her pleas and interceded on my behalf. I was not old enough to offer an opinion on what was happening then, but at around eight or nine, I was more than confident that there had been no divine intervention. I prefer to believe that as I grew older and stronger, my health improved naturally.

I do not remember the childhood reanimations except one. The revivification at age five was the last pre-teen interruption of what should have been a one-way trip on the river Styx. After a very arduous day of seizures and fevers, the house-calling doctor told my mother that I would not live through the night.

The family gathered at my home for the deathwatch. I did not disappoint the audience. Sometime during the early evening, after the most violent attack, I stopped breathing. The doctor covered me with a sheet, candles were lit, and the wailing and prayers began. The cacophony of wails and lamentations apparently frightened me back to life. I threw off the sheets and ran out the door. My father and uncles who were not caught up in the excessive caterwauling chased me down and brough me back into the house. None of those present were amazed, except for the very few that were unfamiliar with my penchant for cheating death, including the attending doctor.

My mother's vow still had a couple of years of tenure left. Here I was, a boy with pigtails wearing a dress (an ugly one at that) andinfinitely embarrassed. Ibloodied many a nose and lips defending my dignity dealing with insensitive school bullies. Since my fighting skills and physique did not match my rage nor did the mane of hair give me Samson like strength, I bled more than a few times myself.

Sometimes, when strangers, usually women,praised me with, "*Hay que nena linda.*" ("Oh, what a cute little girl") I would angrily respond by lifting the damn robe, exposing myself and screaming, "Soy nene!"(I'm a boy!) By the way, when I became a little more sentient, I insisted on wearing pants under the habit. Years later, Johnny Cash's song, "A Boy Named Sue" became one of my favorites since it reminded me of what I went through as a boy wearing long hair and a tasseled frock. That was long before long hair was fashionable or acceptable for men and boys.

My father and I (wearing the habit)
My long hair in pigtails behind my back

Case Histories

"Life is stressful, dear. That's why they say "Rest In Peace."
—*David Mazzucchelli*

In my research I looked for case histories that were a closer match to my own Lazarus experiences. That is the primary reason why I'm highlighting the case of Pablo Picasso's delivery and resurrection second to my own. The Spanish artist's birth ordeal closely matches my first escape from the jaws of death at birth.

Pablo Picasso 1881-1973

Spain 1881- Pablo was declared still born by the midwife who then placed him on a table and went to care for his mother who was in distress. His uncle, Don Salvador, and also a doctor, was present at the birthing, but he did not assist in the procedure. It is not clear why, but he went to where the baby lay. He may have noted a twitch or some sign of life and began to blow cigar smoke in the baby's face, which reportedly made him cry and breathe. That birth, so similar to my own sparked an interest in learning more about Pablo. The uncle was credited with saving the infant's life. Coincidentally, the uncle's name translates to "Savior." It intrigued me that the same method was used to help revive me. It appears that blowing cigar smoke on apparently dead babies was a common medical practice, at least from 1881, when Picasso was born to 1945, when I was born, a span of at least 64 years. That is my conclusion not the result of any medical documents or research. I certainly hope that modern resuscitation methods do not include cigar smoke. I found it surprising that very few of the many Picasso biographies mention his problematic arrival.

At the end of my research, I concluded that there were only two things that connected us. First we shared Spanish ancestry and second, the way we were introduced to the world. That was it. He became a masterful and prolific artist in several art forms. He was creating masterpieces before he was ten. I cannot even draw a stick figure. He was passionate about bull fighting; I saw one and hated it due to the cruelty and the unfairness. The bull can't win. it is pierced repeatedly by picadors. Some say to anger the bull but I believe it is done to weaken it via loss of blood. Even if it flips the matador and avoids the sword thrust, the poor animal is still shot. I still have a chance to match him in longevity - He lived to the age of 92. – *Pablo Picasso – A Life From Beginning to End copyright 2020 by Hourly History*. https://www.pablopicasso.org/picasso-facts.jsp

Saved By the Cigar Jul 8, 2008, | By Jack Bettridge

"Here's a novel form of mouth-to-mouth resuscitation. Apparently, when Pablo Picasso was born in 1881, he wasn't breathing, and the midwife gave him up as stillborn. A quick-thinking and cigar-smoking uncle had other ideas, however. He leaned over and blew smoke into young Pablo's face, causing him to cry and, so, breathe deeply. Mention that next time someone harangues you about health concerns and cigars. This is one case where a cigar saved a life and made the world safe for those crazy paintings of women with two noses and their eyes pointing in different directions."

- Jack Bettridge https://www.cigaraficionado.com/article/saved-by-the-cigar-242

Whoever was smoking a cigar in my home when I was born must have known the famed artist's history.

Officially Declared Dead Again... and Again

*"Dying is a very simple thing. I've looked at death and really
I know. If I should have died it would have been very easy for
me, Quite the easiest thing I ever did. But the people at home
do not realize that. They suffer a thousand times more."*
—Ernest Hemingway

My childhood sickly and dying days were all on my home island. The family eventually moved to the mainland and my teen years proved almost as hazardous.

During a gymnastics event, I attempted a back somersault, landed on my head instead of gracefully on my feet and remained comatose for three days. My aunt, who worked at a hospital watched as the EMTs took my blood pressure. She was amazed that it was close to zero. I recovered and was back home in a few days. There was one possible repercussion that would affect me weeks later. Details in "Close Calls" chapter

 At 16, I went to bed healthy but woke up paralyzed from the waist down, cause - unknown. After a week or so, I gained some use of my legs and hobbled around on crutches, then graduated to a cane. The inexplicable paralysis disappeared after a month or so. A medical diagnosis was suggested much later in life – details to follow.

I've survived five bouts of pneumonia, the full spectrum of childhood ailments, and horrific near fatal accidents in cars and motorcycles, SCUBA diving, Falls from ladders, Almost drowning twice, and more. Strangely I never got the flu and declined yearly flu shots most of my life. That is, until COVID 19 made its appearance. Considering my age and underlying conditions already developed in 2019, I chose the better part of valor and received all vaccines and boosters. It is now 2023 and I have never gotten COVID nor the regular annual version of the flu.

When drafted and marched off to Vietnam, I wondered if my death-defying aura would protect me from bullets, grenades, mortars, or bombs. I escaped unscathed while many of my friends did not. I was also a law enforcement officer for 25 years and avoided serious injury despite confronting armed felons and having a shotgun pointed directly at my face. I remained calm and managed to talk myself out of that frightful situation and moved far enough away to call for backup. Details to follow in the chapter labeled "Close Calls."

In 1996, I joined a longevity study run by NIH in Johns Hopkins Hospital, Baltimore, Maryland. The study requires visiting the hospital every three years and staying for three days. The frequency of visits increases to every two years after reaching 65. At 80, participants are required to visit yearly. Not sure what happens if you're still alive at 90. I jokingly say, every other week.

Studies include MRIs, X-rays, biopsies, scans, heart & lung screenings, mental acuity, bone density, gait, stress tests and a host of other examinations. Over the years, the phlebotomists have withdrawn several pints of blood. They even photograph your taste buds as you continue to age. Participants agree to act as human guinea pigs in order for researchers to study human longevity. If they discover a problem, subjects are advised to notify their own primary care physician. The study does not allow for intervention or treatments by NIH (National Institute of Health), should they discover a previously undiagnosed ailment. A bonus that is appreciated and well known among the geriatric group is that participants tend to live longer than the average population. Most likely due to early warning of developing illnesses. Potentially fatal ailments are not so calamitous if discovered early. Study subjects also tend to take better care of themselves and are more aware of preventive health care, supplements, nutrition, and exercise.

In the early days of participation, I asked "If there are signs of developing dementia, do you let the participant know? They said "No." A few years later, the NIH changed that exemption and now they will advise if there appears to be a decline in mental acuity. Dementia happens to be the only ailment I fear. Not because of my personal suffering, I will probably not even realize that anything is wrong, but because I do not want to burden any member of my family with the agonizing duty of caring for me or anyone in that miserable condition.

The one obligation the study insists on is that a participant's body has to be delivered to the researchers packed in ice within 24 hours. The body is returned to the family (if they want it), after an autopsy and/or biopsies of major organs. They want to verify the exact cause of death which is the primary goal of the life-long study.

I joined that select group in 1996. Over the years, I have been probed, screened, scanned, and tested by dozens of doctors in every field of medicine, but I never thought of seeking an explanation for my connection to the Lazarus effect. I had not yet become aware that the descriptive phrase had been coined.

Two visits ago, I asked. They were not astounded, nor surprised at my story except for the frequency of near-death events. Most Lazarus Effect subjects do it only once or twice and always due to one specific event, heart attack, stroke, or trauma.

There are stories of children who fall through ice and are underwater for hours, yet some recover with no adverse effects. The traumatic shock and water temperature forces their metabolism to slow down, and there is no evidence of a heartbeat. It may stop completely in some cases. The oxygen remaining in their lungs may be doled out slowly with the brain getting priority. Later research indicates other conditions may be necessary to preserve the body and organs. The temperature of the water is a factor, and some other cases involve snow or ice.

The doctors conducting the longevity study told me that the same thing could happen to children who cry so much they cannot breathe so the body shuts down to biologically "re-boot." The body relaxes and when settled, comes back to life hopefully before much harm is done. The same is possible with severe seizures. I also questioned the doctors at the NIH study about my paralysis as a teen. They suggested that it had probably been a virus that affected my spinal cord causing temporary paralysis. My immune system eventually did its job and evicted the harmful unwanted guests.

I remained "death free" for quite a few decades until the last few years.

About seven years ago, for unknown reasons, I "fell out." I collapsed and was so disoriented that I was unable to even dial 911. I tried several times, but just could not manage it. My phone had emergency contacts in large letters, and I managed to push one button that called my oldest grandson. I had trouble speaking but managed to mumble "Help.' He understood that I was in trouble, and he called rescue and his sister. Both my grandkids arrived before the rescue unit. Also fortunate since my door was locked but they both had keys. They found me on the floor, barely able to talk. Rescue arrived, and the medic's first words while checking my blood pressure were, "I don't know how you're still talking or conscious." After a few hours in the Emergency room, there was no definitive diagnosis. A stroke and heart attack were ruled out. Blood Pressure was restored, I fully recovered and was sent home. That event was a prelude to a grimmer crisis about a year later.

The most recent and perhaps most funereal Lazarus event occurred in May of 2017. Despite all the testing during the NIH study and my attempt to maintain a healthy lifestyle, I still suffered a massive heart attack and flat-lined twice. (Two more "deaths?") I was in a coma for eleven days. Doctors and family discussed "pulling the plug" but my history of reanimations gave them pause. Also due to my frequent acts of renascence, I make it a point to NOT sign a DNR (Do Not Resuscitate form).

When I regained consciousness, the first person I saw was a young ICU doctor. After they removed the breathing tube, my first question was, *"How bad was it?"* He did not say anything but pantomimed chest compressions and held up two fingers, indicating twice My first thought was, *"Wow, two more."*

Since my parents did not keep tabs on the frequency of events, I'll never know for sure how many times I've managed to re-ignite the pilot light with or without medical assistance. I can be sure of at least four documented or verified events, The ones that are beyond recall are the several that occurred during infancy between my birth and the one at five years of age. I just know that my mother said it was often. It is impossible to convert "often" to a number, but I can guess at the very least four more. That brings the {inaccurate) total to 8, but easily could have been twice that many. On my "Close Calls" list there are about 15 more that almost qualify, but they do not really count as Lazarus events.

The acute myocardial infarction should not have happened. It was preventable had I listened to some members of my family or reacted to my own body's warnings that something was wrong. For four days, I felt an annoying discomfort in my chest. I have read enough health precautions to know better and was well aware of the signals indicating a possible heart problem. It was a case of pride and stubbornness.

I was running three miles at least three times a week and believed I was in perfect health. I just did not accept that I could have a heart on the edge of failure. Considering my personal history, I was also overly confident. Reminds me of Alfred E. Neumans' favorite comeback: "What, me worry?"

I put up with the discomfort for three days until my son told me that I looked terrible (not exactly in those words). I agreed because I really did feel like crap. I finally made the decision to head to the nearest emergency room. Drove myself (foolishly) and when I arrived, went to the receptionist and told her that I believed I was having a cardiac problem. She told me to sign in and that is all I remember. I collapsed before I could sign the form she gave me. A thought just occurred: It appears that my unique situation includes a delaying factor that kept me going until I was in an emergency room where I could get immediate assistance. Had it happened just a few minutes earlier in city traffic, I would not have been the only casualty.

I was instantly unconscious and therefore have no idea what anyone did. What I know now comes from the medical report covering the action taken, by whom, the procedures performed, the severity of the problem and the length of time in "code." The resuscitation effort by doctors lasted for 85 minutes. I went into cardiac arrest twice during that hour and twenty-five minutes under critical cardiac care. Due to the massive heart failure, and the lack of blood flow, some organs were damaged. My kidneys suffered acute tubular necrosis. There is a

40% mortality rate if that condition is not resolved. If it persists, life expectancy is a year. It has now been over six years since that event and so far, there have been no renal ill effects.

Most of the younger family members had heard the stories of my past but on May 16 of that year they witnessed my Lazarus act themselves. This time however, I believe their caring, attention and support were the prime reasons for my survival and/or recovery. Oh, yes, the doctors did a fabulous job too.

I survived the seven-year death sentence given me by doctors in my infancy and now I must deal with another established mortality prediction or timetable. The heart incident caused serious and irreversible injury to my heart, lowering its ejection fraction (LVEF) to 26%. The mortality rate for those with an Ejection Fraction in the 20's is about 3 years. My low ejection fraction is the result of the heart suffering 25% necrosis. In other words, a quarter of my heart is dead. I've already used up the three years of the allotted time. As of this writing, I am approaching the 6th anniversary of those two Lazarus episodes. I may need to provide an update on or around my expanded expiry date. Until then I'll continue my merry way in the hope that my appointment with the grim reaper is delayed at least one or more times.

I have been provided with "early warning" protective measures. I carry a first alert button around my neck most of the time. During the night at bedside, there is a cell phone type device in constant contact with Biometrics, the company that provided my implanted defribilator. Should the device detect a problem and the defibrillator kicks in, a signal is sent and hopefully assistance will arrive in time. I also have a CGM (Continuous Glucose Monitoring) system in my arm. It rings an alarm if my glucose goes critical, either high or low, Low levels kill you quickly and high levels kill too, but just takes a little longer.

Coincidentally, I had a life insurance policy for a hundred thousand dollars that lapsed exactly a month after my heart failure. It expired before I did and as was to be expected, the insurance company refused to renew it. The beneficiary was my brother but he was not disappointed…I think.

Cold Water Drowning &
Frozen Alive

*"Time," the Captain said, "is not what you think." He sat down
next to Eddie. "Dying? Not the end of everything. We think it is.
But what happens on earth is only the beginning."—Mitch Albom*

The average age of those experiencing resuscitation is 60 or more. There
are also well-known cases of children and young adults regaining life
after drowning, especially in cold water or frozen solid in snow/ice or
other very cold environments.

This type of Lazarus Effect is more often experienced by children and
younger adults.

John Smith 2015

A true unique drowning case was adapted into the movie
Breakthrough in 2019

A boy from Guatemala was adopted as a baby by Brian and Joyce Smith.
They named him John. He had a normal childhood, enjoyed basketball,
and had close friends, including a girlfriend named Abby. In 2015 at
age 14, he and two friends, Josh and Rieger decided to go play on MLK
day at an apparently frozen lake near his home. While playing all three
fell through the ice.

Rescue units arrived and managed to get Josh and Rieger out of the water
to safety with no complications. John, however, had sunk to the bottom of
the muddy water. One rescuer now considered this as a recovery effort rather
than a rescue mission since John was unconscious and had been under for a
while. A fellow rescuer was able to find the third unresponsive boy who had
been submerged already for fifteen minutes and had not received CPR for
at least twenty minutes and had no readable pulse for another twenty-five
minutes en route to the hospital.

The emergency room doctor on duty at the hospital who is also the boy's girlfriend's father tells the mother to say goodbye to her son. Surprisingly, the boy regains a pulse when the mother moves to his bedside. The mother, a devout Christian, was praying by his side when the pulse was detected. She believes in miracles and was confident that God will intervene to save her son. Opposing opinions on John's chance of revival are voiced, but the ER physician, who is also an expert in drowning cases, expresses his scientifically based view that the boy will not last the night. However, if he does survive, there will be massive and possible neurological damage to his brain after being without oxygen for an extensive length of time. The boy's father, not as full of hope and faith as the mother, feared the worst.

Some of the information comes from the movie's plot story, but later research indicates that John had no pulse for over an hour, and he was technically dead. "No spontaneous respirations. No heart tones. In essence, he was cold, and he was dead. "He was gone, said Dr. Kent Sutterer, the ER doctor on duty that day."-*CBN*

"…The only factors medically that were really in John's favor is that this was a cold-water drowning," said Dr. Jeremy Garrett …He (also) said that lowering the body temperature can preserve brain function, but that it "really shouldn't have worked in John's case." This is because the lake water was only 40 degrees and John's body temperature only dropped to 88 degrees, which isn't cold enough to adequately protect the brain.

"Usually you'd like it to be colder and you'd like the victim to be smaller actually," said Dr. Garrett, "because what you really need to have happen is for the brain to get cold before the blood flow stops to the brain. So, for John's brain to have gotten cold to be protected from the lack of blood flow and the lack of oxygen really is a miracle in itself, if that did anything here." -*Cincinnati.com*

https://www.historyvshollywood.com/reelfaces/breakthrough/
https://www.imdb.com/title/tt7083526/plotsummary/

This "return from the dead" story was adapted into the movie *"Breakthrough,"* released in 2019. Although some events were slightly altered for dramatic effect it is a true story. The dramatic changes revolve around the mother's religious devotion and she and her pastor give more credit to divine intervention than to medical science. Despite the difference of opinion in crediting which side had more influence in determining the outcome, it is an entertaining and thought-provoking movie. John eventually fully recovered, finished school, and went to college to become a minister, proving that there was no permanent damage to his brain.

Justin Smith 2016

As I worked on this book. I took a break and went to an appointment at the audiology clinic in the VA Hospital. When I sat down for a talk with the hearing specialist prior to the examination, he mentioned that my record stated that I was a writer. I answered in the affirmative and then he asked, "What do you write about?" I mentioned that I was currently working on a book about the Lazarus Effect. He lit up and said, "I know someone who experienced that." It was then my turn to light up. What better source than a real doctor who could provide firsthand information?

The story he told me was one of the most interesting, and, if I were a true believer, one of the most "miraculous," in my selection of case histories. I must say, even more unusual than some of my triumphs avoiding permanent death.

A young man of 25 years was out at a bar on a snowy, and extremely cold day, near his home. in Hazleton, PA. (Coincidentally, I owned property in that town.) He was advised that the weather was getting worse and should leave early. It seems that he slipped on the ice and fell into a snowbank during the walk home and knocked himself out. Witnesses claim he left the bar at about 9:30 PM. He did not make it home that night. The father woke up in the morning and discovered his son was not in his room. His father checked his phone and found calls from Justin's girlfriend asking about his whereabouts. She did not know where he was either.

The concerned dad got in his car and went to look for his son. He found him shortly thereafter, buried in a snowbank, with only his feet sticking out of the deep snow. The temperature was 4 degrees below zero. The young man was frozen solid. Mr. Smith called for a rescue unit but when the EMT team arrived, they covered the body believing he was dead.

They even radioed dispatchers that the young man had apparently been dead for a long time. He had no heartbeat, no temperature and not breathing. At the hospital there was also no indication of brain activity.

In the hospital, the ER physician, Doctor Coleman, declined to pronounce him, since the usual practice is not to "call" a cold body. He wanted to wait until the body was warm. Hopeful that there was still a chance, they decided to try a cutting-edge hypothermia treatment by draining the blood, filtering out the CO_2 that had accumulated, warming the blood and pumping it back into the body.

At one point as the body warmed, the brain showed some signs of function. Every method of resuscitation was tried and probably some that were unconventional. Whatever they tried apparently worked since Justin made an almost complete recovery except for losing all his toes and both pinky fingers as a result of hypothermia.

My doctor at the VA showed me a YouTube video and we took a little time to watch it. When I got home, I found that YouTube has several videos describing this episode, and while some of them have slightly different versions of the event, the minimal variations do not negate the authenticity of this quite unusual Lazarus Effect. I have listed some of the links to the videos that tell the story from assorted points of view, including doctors, parents, first responders, reporters, and Justin himself. The facts are that Justin was frozen solid for ten to twelve hours, no oxygen, no heartbeat and still recovered except for losing a few fingers and toes. This young man's resuscitation and recovery were more amazing than most of the ones I researched including my own. The links are not necessary to find the videos. Just connect to Youtube and search for John Smith or Justin Smith with key words such as "frozen alive".

https://www.youtube.com/watch?v=BGwxAitvJT8
https://www.youtube.com/watch?v=uT0DaoZyf3I
https://www.youtube.com/results?search_
query=justin+smith+frozen+man
https://www.youtube.com/watch?v=XIV7TJwI-_s
https://www.youtube.com/watch?v=CK1lude7gjM

Cryogenics

"If we really think that home is elsewhere and that this life is a 'wandering to find home,' why should we not look forward to the arrival?" —C. S. Lewis

It may be interesting and important to note that lowering body temperature on patients that are very ill or scheduled for serious surgery has become an accepted practice. The procedure helps healing and speeds recovery.

Events such as Justin Smith's have also given credence to a theory about resuscitating frozen bodies. Experiments are underway that freeze people soon after being declared dead after the heart, lungs and brain cease to function. The cryogenic process must begin as close to the official declaration of death as possible to minimize cell damage which begins soon after the last breath. Due to the expense and difficulty of freezing a whole body, two thirds of the hopeful candidates elect to preserve only the head or the brain. Since most of those who long for immortality via the science of cryogenics are old, they do not want to be brought back into a body suffering from the various diseases that accompany aging such as diabetes, arthritis, atrophied muscles, and whatever fatal disease was most responsible for their demise. There are some famous people who allegedly had their heads fozen and stored. One of the sources indicated that Walt Disney was not one.

The cryogenic storage idea was in its infancy and not quite ready to accept participants. There are some clinics now, but most are in Britain. It appears to be a growing business. There are about 250 bodies that are already cryopreserved in the US with about 1500 more that have agreed to participate in the process when their time comes. This is activity since 2014. Earlier attempts in the '60s and '70s ended in failure and the frozen bodies were disposed of. There does not appear to be much confidence of any success soon enough to produce the results offered. The experiment has a long way to go before stored remains can be revived safely. The idea is currently not economically feasible. That problem will not stop people who want to come back to life someday, from signing up. Most participants are wealthy and may not be concerned over the cost of returning to life. Those who are pro cryonics maintain that the brain does not need to remain active in order to preserve memory. That belief is contrary to popular opinion. Future improvements in AI technology may help in storing memory ingrams that can be uploaded after thawing out the corpse.

Frozen Bodies Brought Back to Life? Cryogenics and the Science of Immortality | Documentary - YouTube Cryonics - Wikipedia "The Eternal Promise". The Verge. 2015. Archived from the original on 2023-03-26. Retrieved 2021-01-22.

Other Lazarus Cases

"Every man must do two things alone; he must do his own believing and his own dying. —Martin Luther

There are scores of cases where some have "come back to life" after apparently expiring. A recent study examined medical reports on the phenomenon in the years between 1982 and 2018, found over 65 individuals who came back to life. Eighteen of them made a complete recovery after escaping from the grim reaper.

These are documented cases, but researchers believe that the event is more prevalent. It is possible that some doctors do not report some cases to avoid embarrassment or malpractice lawsuits. Many of the patients died permanently after briefly showing signs of life. That report covers only 1982 to 2018 but that does not mean that there were none before or after those years. For various reasons including malpractice lawsuits doctors did not concern themselves too much or often over spontaneous resuscitations. Today there is more emphasis on taking more care in "calling" permanent terminations. I, for one, am glad that my cardiac doctors in 2017, continued working on me for over 85 minutes until they were sure I was stable. Quite unlike those practitioners (?) who did not even bother spending a few minutes before telling my father to "take him home, he's dead" back in the late 40's.

There are way too many cases to list here and I've excluded some that died permanently shortly after initial or several attempts at resuscitation. Interested readers can find more stories and videos by searching using the key word Lazarus followed by effect, syndrome, or heart.

August 5, 2013, Bellbrook Ohio A 37-year-old man was not breathing normally and was unresponsive. No pulse was detected by rescue EMS who tried CPR. They were able to restore enough heartbeats to take him to the emergency room. He again went into cardiac arrest for 45 minutes some hours later at the Kettering Medical Center. He was pronounced dead after efforts to revive him did not succeed. His son went to see his allegedly dead father but saw a heartbeat on the still connected heart monitor. Doctors resumed CPR and the last attempt proved successful for the patient. *Ohio man pronounced dead comes back to life after 45 minutes*- Author:*WFAA Staff Pub:3:47 PM CDT August 21, 2013*

An 11-month-old girl in ICU kept the caretakers extremely busy. They tried aggressive CPR, four shocks to her heart, seven doses of adrenaline and multiple bags of IV fluids. But the baby remained flatlined with no pulse. She was declared dead. The pediatrician allowed the parents a little time with their infant, before bagging her. After 15 minutes the mother asked to hold the baby and a breathing tube was removed. Then something incredible happened. Shortly after the tube was extracted, she began to breathe on her own, and her heart began to beat. The doctor said he had never seen anything like this. Even though the girl stabilized, she died four months later in a critical care clinic. The majority of similar Lazarus Phenomenon cases eventually pass away sometime later, about one third make complete recoveries. According to some surveys this miracle is more common than generally suspected. It may be underreported because of legal issues. -*Science Adam Hoffman March 31, 2016*

It seems that the most difficult decisions for ICU doctors and other medical experts are when to stop CPR or remove life support equipment, and also how long to maintain careful observation. In some cases, like mine, the only clue was a barely noticeable twitch of a pinky.

Still births appear to be more common than generally expected. Out of 4 million babies born every year, almost ten percent need resuscitation. There were probably considerably more in the era that I arrived, so my event was not that unusual. The Neonatal, a 1987 Resuscitation Program, developed a plan to help medical personnel identify babies born in distress and react quickly and properly to reanimate and save the infant. (*I wonder if cigar smoke is part of the procedure.*) Fortunately, I was able to survive without need of that program. Also, very fortunate for children born after that year because now there is at least a plan or more concern for babies who previously were discarded as unsavable.

Talkad s. Raghuveer, MD, and Austin J. Cox, MD - Am Fam Physician. 2011;83(8):911-918

One of the older reported cases listed a woman named Countess Emma. She married the rich Earl of Mount Edgcumbe in 1761. The countess apparently died shortly after the wedding. She was buried wearing a valuable ring. A sexton (church employee – bell ringer, caretaker, and sometimes grave digger), spying on the family noticed the ring during burial preparations. He returned after dark, dug up the coffin and in the process, the countess "woke up." The terrorized grave robber ran off at the unexpected resurrection. The countess then climbed out of the coffin and walked a half mile back to her estate. Her unexpected appearance shocked all who believed she had died. The route she took back to her home is now known as the Countess's Path.' Emma died permanently in 1807. https://historycollection.com/author/alexa/

A more recent back from the dead story is a man from Venezuela who was declared dead and moved to the morgue. Carlos Camejo, 33, was declared dead after a highway accident and taken to the morgue, where examiners began an autopsy only to realize something was amiss when he started bleeding. They quickly sought to stitch up the incision on his face.

"I woke up because the pain was unbearable," Camejo said, according to a report on Friday in leading local newspaper *El Universal.*

His grieving wife turned up at the morgue to identify her husband's body only to find him moved into a corridor -- and alive.

Reuters could not immediately reach hospital officials to confirm the events. But Camejo showed the newspaper his facial scar and a document ordering the autopsy. – Reuters

"The Lazarus phenomenon is a grossly underreported event," notes Maxillofacial Surgeon Dr. Vaibhav Sahni *Sage Journals 2016*

Cousin Ed

While editing the book prior to publication, an incident occurred in my family that deserves mention as it is an event clearly related to Lazarus Syndrome. A cousin, 10 years younger than I, went to the hospital for a surgical procedure that included bypass surgery on his left leg. Lower extremity bypass is considered major surgery and carries significant risks depending on the severity of the blockage and the length of the incision. In my cousin's case, the cut was from the ankle to the groin. The surgery itself was successful; however, he suffered 4 heart attacks in 3 hours in the ICU recovery room. He was resuscitated all four times.

The doctors said the prognosis was not very comforting. The family had a choice. Heart bypass surgery was indicated, but it would be extremely dangerous in his condition, especially after the damage to his heart caused by the repeated heart attacks. His chances of survival were slim with or without further surgical intervention, but the chance of survival was slightly higher if the bypass attempts worked. He needed a quadruple bypass. The family agreed to the attempt to repair the blockages. It took six more hours to complete the arduous task, but when it was over, he was still alive. He is now in an induced coma after two days. His condition is still considered critical, but we are all hopeful that after a long rest, he will improve.

Here is a short list of reported Lazarus Effect cases with various recovery and survival timelines.

Only about 63 (*this number has increased since this story was first reported*) cases of Lazarus syndrome have been documented in medical journals. Some of these cases have made it into the news headlines, such as:

In Ohio, a 37-year-old man collapsed at home. In the hospital, his heart stopped, and he was pronounced dead despite 45 minutes of CPR. Several minutes later, his family noticed his monitor showed a heart rhythm. A week later, he was well enough to go home.

A 20-year-old woman in Detroit was declared dead after 30 minutes of CPR. She was taken to the funeral home where staff discovered she was breathing. She was treated in the hospital but died permanently 2 months later.

A 23-year-old British man was pronounced dead after failed CPR. About 30 minutes later, a priest gave him last rites and noticed he was breathing. He died in the hospital 2 days later.

https://www.healthline.com/health/lazarus-syndrome

Vedamurthy Adhiyaman a geriatric doctor developed an interest in the Lazarus Effect after involvement with a case in the early 2000s, He and his team did CPR on a man in his 70s for about 15 minutes with no positive results.

"There isn't any definite time frame for how long you should attempt CPR before you stop," says Adhiyaman. "It really varies on a case-by-case basis." The doctor did not make the call immediately; a member of his team told the family the patient was dead. It appears that events were not that clear. "After about 15 to 20 minutes, he started breathing," recalls Adhiyaman. "But he remained unconscious in a coma for the next two days until he died on day three."

The family sued the doctor for "substandard care." "It was around that time that I began researching this phenomenon, because I had to show evidence that these things do happen," he says.

The doctor researched medical records and found 38 cases of Lazarus Phenomenon which was enough to clear him of negligence.

Dr. Adhiyaman published his review in the *Journal of the Royal Society of Medicine.* He found that on average, these patients returned from death's door seven minutes after stopping CPR, though close monitoring in many cases was inconsistent. Three patients were left unattended for several minutes, with one making it all the way to the hospital mortuary before being discovered alive.

Adhiyaman's analysis also showed that these positive outcomes were not really affected by the duration of CPR or the amount of time it took for patients to auto-resuscitate.

Coming back from the experience is rare. In 2010, a team at McGill University conducted a review of reports and found only 32 cases of the Lazarus Phenomenon since 1982. In the same year, a German team found 45 articles on the subject. Many of the same cases appear in both reports.

Plus, recent reports suggest that the event may not be recorded. A 2013 study showed that about half of all French emergency room physicians admitted dealing with a case of autoresuscitation during their career, while according to a 2012 survey more than one-third of Canadian critical care doctors reported handled at least one case. It is possible that some MDs do not make official reports to avoid troubling legal and professional consequences. There is also the problem of privacy concerns.

Patrick J. Oneill Phd. MD. FACS of Arizona Trauma and Acute Care Consortium (AZTRACC) on a YouTube video details various facts of the "rare but real" Lazarus Effect. The doctor does a better job on a YouTube Video, describing the Lazarus Syndrome than I can. He details several events, some of which he participated in. He explains some suspected causes. One possibility is called Auto Peep, or *positive end-expiratory pressure* caused by the buildup of air due to not exhaling completely before taking the next breath. Air is trapped when the patient can't breathe out and the breathing process is limited, interfering with blood returning to the heart, another factor may involve the infusion of drugs into the patient but there is a delayed reaction when the drugs "catch up" and create a sudden accumulated effect. *Patrick J. Oneill Ph.D. MD. FACS of Arizona Trauma and Acute Care Consortium (AZTRACC)YouTube*

Some experts advise that CPR that goes on for longer than usual should be paused for about ten seconds to prevent the above described "Peep" (*positive end-expiratory pressure*).

Another related term mentioned by Dr. Patrick J. Oneill is the Lazarus Taxon which refers to the reappearance of fossil records after a period of extinction. This may mean that a species believed to be extinct is discovered in a much later time period, it appears that even animals, prehistoric and current appear to benefit from spontaneous revivification.

During my research I found this advisory:

A note from Cleveland Clinic

"While the Lazarus effect is rare, CPR and attempts to save someone's life happen in the medical world every day. So, reading about this phenomenon can be a good reminder to learn more about life support and end-of-life care. Talk to your provider about your options and how to put your preferences into writing." – *Cleveland Clinic, Ohio My Cleveland Clinic.org*

Dr. Adhiyaman published his review in the *Journal of the Royal Society of Medicine.* He found that on average, these patients returned from death's door seven minutes after stopping CPR, though close monitoring in many cases was inconsistent. Three patients were left unattended for several minutes, with one making it all the way to the hospital mortuary before being discovered alive.

The great majority of patients died soon after auto-resuscitation, but 35 percent were eventually sent home with no significant neurological consequences. Adhiyaman's analysis also showed that these positive outcomes were not really affected by the duration of CPR or the amount of time it took for patients to auto-resuscitate. *Adhiyaman V, Adhiyaman S and Sundaram R. The Lazarus phenomenon. Journal of the Royal Society of Medicine, 2007. 100(12): 552-557.*

Another issue to be considered in Lazarus Effect cases is organ donor timeline. Do they act too quickly to harvest needed organs or wait too long?

A story on Good Morning America (GMA) featured 13-year-old Trenton Mckinley who suffered seven skull fractures in an accident. His heart stopped for 15 minutes and was declared brain dead. Believing that he was beyond hope, his parents signed papers to donate their son's organs. Five organ recipients were expecting Trenton's usable organs. The boy spontaneously began breathing and made a quick recovery. He regained full cognition within 48 hours, While the family called it a miracle, the doctor treating him suggested that uninjured areas of the boy's brain "re-wired and took up the slack" from the damaged portions of his brain.

Re-reading, I just noticed that Johns Hopkins University Hospital may not agree to organ sharing. I forgot that they have first dibs on my remains due to the longevity study I belong to. There may be parts they won't need for their final evaluation. I wonder if any parts that continue servicing another person would count as remaining alive. I believe there have been movies based on that premise.

The Lazarus Phenomenon, Explained: Why Sometimes, the Deceased Are Not Dead, Yet

What does CPR have to do with the curious case of clinically dead patients coming "back to life"? Adam Hoffman March 31, 2016

The previously cited Doctor Patrick J Oneill mentioned in his presentation that patients believed to be dead should be checked for "end tidal CO2" or tested for exhaled Carbon Dioxide which indicates remaining metabolic function. The premise is that since CO2 is produced as a by product or waste after people breathe in oxygen, the process of breathing is still functioning but at a lower level.

Ecuador: A woman was removed from her coffin during her wake after her family heard banging from inside the casket 5 hours into the wake. The woman was rushed back to the hospital. Government agencies are investigating.

Comatose states

"There is no hell quite like mourning the loss of a loved one who is still alive" —Pinterest

Terri Schiavo

This case was not a Lazarus Effect situation, but it highlights the problems that families and legal authorities encounter when a person falls into an irreversible "persistent vegetative state." In 1990, at 26 years old, the young lady's heart stopped beating but was resuscitated. Unfortunately, due to lack of oxygen, suffered severe brain damage. She fell into a comatose state and after two and a half months displayed no improvement. Doctors diagnosed her as being in a persistent vegetative state. They continued several therapeutic efforts, speech, physical and occupational, plus other methods considered experimental with no positive results. The procedures failed to produce any level of awareness.

Eight years later in 1998, her husband Michael, filed a suit in a Florida court to remove her feeding tube as is allowed under Florida statutes. Her parents opposed the intervention. The court, however, agreed with the husband that she would not have wanted to just exist in a comatose state. After the court's order the feeding tube was removed on April 24, 2001. A few days later feeding was restarted. About 4 years later a county judge ordered the tube removed again. Removal was delayed by several appeals and the involvement of Federal Courts. The federal courts eventually agreed with the original court order and Schiavo's tube was removed on March 18, 2005. She died 13 days later. This case was recently featured in an HBO documentary. The case eventually involved not only federal courts but Congress, the Senate and even the President of the United States. There were numerous demostrations and rallies throughout the country pitting pro-life supporters versus pro-choice groups. *Between Life and Death: Terri Schiavo's Story Peacock, MSNBC Dec 3, 2023*

Hutchinson, Kansas. September 1984. The following does not technically qualify as a resuscitation, but it was an event that, to me, was a fate worse than death and much more disturbing than any situation that befell me. An 18-year college student, Sarah Scantlin was walking home with her best friend, Laurie when she was struck by a car and sent flying into the air, before hitting the ground, she was hit again by a car going in the opposite direction, Sarah suffered severe multiple injuries to her spine and head. She was transported via helicopter to an intensive care unit 45 minutes away. Doctors performed numerous surgical procedures on her spine and brain including cutting out parts of Broca's area in the frontal lobe which is also the area linked to speech production. Sarah never regained consciousness and remained in a coma for 20 years; longer than anyone else on record. The family chose to continue treatment despite the high cost which nearly drove them into bankruptcy.

Her best friend Laurie visited her regularly during the twenty-year span. In a January 2005 visit, Laurie found Sarah awake and talking, but with difficulty. She was unable to move due to her joints having fused during her long comatose state. Sarah was unaware of the passage of time and did not quite understand why her friend looked so old. The family was overjoyed that their daughter had woken up. The YOUTUBE episode provides more details and touching moments. Sarah continued her care at the center she had lived in for the last 20 years. She lived for another eleven years.

Most hospitals today give patients a choice of what they want done should they require resuscitation or extreme efforts to maintain life. The DNR form is usually signed by the patient but a spouse or relative can also be involved in the decision. This may also help make the desired decision in situations where the patient enters a persistent vegetative state. Sometimes a delay is warranted if the patient is an organ donor and has viable organs. To prevent involving the courts, most people should consider a medical power of attorney that is able to intercede if a possible patient does not want to be kept in a vegetative state on a long-term basis.

Even though I've shown a tendency to recover from serious medical events, my two oldest grandkids have instructions and authority to "pull the plug" if the EEG displays a non-functional brain. At my age, I don't believe I have any organs that anyone else would want. But if needed they can be made available unless they are past the "use by" date.

I've been in a comatose state twice. The first one for about three days and the second, years later, for about eleven days. Neither caused any permanent damage although I now believe that the first one wiped out a portion of some memory. I mentioned this incident in the chapter titled "Close Calls."

Since I've experienced at least two deep comas, I feel qualified to comment on the experience. In the first one I was 15. It lasted only three days and I don't recall anything unusual. In fact, I don't recall anything at all. It was as close as being dead since there is nothing for me to remember that I can document. The second one was a bit different. The cause was a lot more severe than a bump in the head. I actually visited the great beyond for a short while but do not recall any beckoning lights or any paranormal events. Nor did I experience any "out of body" observations. These are usually called NDE's or near-death experiences. Most of mine did not qualify as nearly dead or almost dead but really dead.

I remember dreams though, quite a series of them. They were unusual due to the primary subject of the unconscious adventures. First, most of the dreams featured a particular bank; one in which I did not have an account.

When I leave my house on an errand, I usually head west for one block and make a left turn at the first light. One of the first buildings I notice is a green and white bank. It will remain nameless since there is no need to give them any free publicity. I would see it frequently, sometimes several times a day.

In one dream, I rolled up to the bank in a wheelchair but could not speak with a breathing tube down my throat, which helped me breathe in real life during my comatose state in intensive care. Since I had no voice, I wrote a note asking for a withdrawal. The teller, assuming I could not hear either, wrote a note stating that I did not have an account in their bank. I could not dispute that, so I rolled away.

In another dream, I was waiting in line for service (sans wheelchair) and suffered a medical emergency. When the rescue unit arrived, I was placed on the bank counter to get emergency treatment. I exited the dream without learning the outcome.

The other dreams featured my son and youngest grandson, I would rather not publicize those dreams. They were not controversial but were more of a personal nature that I shared only with them. The odd thing was that those dreams also included the bank in question. Other dreams were more like nightmares. I would see thousands of bugs, more like big roaches crawling on the hospital room walls. Others involved dozens of rats scurrying around on the room's floor. These evolved into hallucinations after awakening allegedly brought about by the infusion of multiple medications.

Another event of note deals with possible neurological activity while unconscious. My oldest granddaughter visited daily. She said that she was surprised when during some visits she would play my favorite songs on her cell phone while holding my hand and I would sometimes squeeze her hand when a particular favorite was playing. She mentioned this to the attending doctors, and they said that was a good sign. I do not remember hearing the songs nor the hand squeezing, but I do not doubt her story.

After treatment and weeks of therapy and being able to travel, the first thing I did was open an account at the bank featured in my dreams. Nothing unusual came of it but I'm hoping it meant something. I also opened an account for my granddaughter who helped take care of my mother and after my problem took care of both of us for months with little or no pay. I will be grateful as long as I live.

There are programs available that depict cases of comatose levels. One HBO Documentary titled "COMA" follows four patients in various stages. The stages include unresponsiveness, early responsiveness, agitation and confusion, and higher level of responsiveness. The more serious stages include minimal responsiveness and permanent vegetative state.

In 1994 a review of 700 patients discovered that none regained any awareness after two years in a permanent vegetative state.

The more I research, The Lazarus Syndrome becomes more gruesome and even more fearsome. At times it is even more difficult to diagnose. There are medical conditions that can challenge the most skilled doctors and even their high-tech equipment.

Benjamin Franklin once said, *"In this world nothing is certain but death and taxes."*

In hospitals, clinics, or hospices, being declared dead is not always an absolute definitive conclusion, as sure as it is supposed to be. Nor is it as easy a decision to make. There are various levels of coma or catatonic stages. Some can even baffle brain scans.

One is Catalepsy, a trance-like state that slows breathing, lowers sensitivity, and makes someone totally immobile. The condition can last from minutes to weeks. It is believed to be a complication from epilepsy and Parkinson's disease.

Another condition appears to be the most dreadful of all. A patient in a condition known as *locked-in* syndrome, is aware of surroundings, but is totally paralyzed except for the muscles that move the eyes.

In 2014, *The Daily Mail* reported on 39-year-old British woman Kate Allatt, who had locked-in syndrome. Ignorant of the lady's situation, doctors declared her brain dead. Medics, family, and friends by her bedside considered when it would be time to pull the plug and terminate life support. Unknown to the attendees, Allatt heard everything that was said near her. Unfortunately, she could not tell them that she was aware but unable to move or draw attention to her immobile condition in any way. Kate Allatt survived her ordeal and became an advocate for stroke victims. "Locked-in syndrome is like being buried alive," said Allatt. "You can think, you can feel, you can hear, but you can communicate absolutely nothing." The Daily Mail.com 2014 *Mail.com 2014* <u>www. Don'tlowetyourexpectations.com www.KateAllatt.com</u>

The lady recovered completely. Has written 3 books and is an advocate for stroke, and comatose patients as well as others.

A Few More Lazarus Cases

Death may be the greatest of all human blessings" – Socrates

Janina Kolkiewicz's heart stopped beating, nor was she breathing. At 91 years of age, she was declared dead Apparaently, she was not ready to go. Eleven hours later, she awoke in the hospital mortuary with a craving for tea and pancakes. As unbelievable as it appears, Kolkiewicz is just one of many believed to have "risen from the dead."- The Associated Press·Posted: Nov 14, 2014

In 2001, aman aged 66,suffered cardiac arrest while undergoing surgery for an abdominal aneurysm. After 17 minutes attempts using CPR, defribilation and drugs, his vital signs did not restart. He was pronounced but ten minutes later the surgeon detected a pulse. The operation resumed and proved successful.

In 2014, a 78-year-old from Mississippiwas declared dead when a hospice nurse found him with no pulse. The next day, he woke up in a body bag at the morgue._- _The Lazarus phenomenon: When the 'dead' come back to life (medicalnewstoday.com)

Some of these stories appear to be more appropriate in horror movies but they are real-life cases of Lazarus Symdrome.

In 2014 a sad storyof an 80-year-old lady who was "frozen alive" in a hospital morgue after being wrongly declared dead.

In the same year, a New York Hospital was blasted for erroneously declaring a woman as brain dead after a drug overdose. The woman "came back to life" soon after arriving in an operating room for organ harvesting.

These types of cases can make one wonder how it is possible to mistakingly declare a person as dead.

There are two types of death: clinical death and biological death. Clinical death is defined as the absence of a pulse, heartbeat, and breathing, while biological death is defined as the absence of brain activity. The Lazarus phenomenon: When the 'dead' come back to life (medicalnewstoday.com)

Looking at these definitions, you might assume that it would be easy to tell when a person is truly deceased, especially in today's medical system where diagnostic equipment, computers, EKGs, EEGs, CAT Scans and other technical tools are in use – but in some cases, it has not been so simple.

Hypothermia can cause heartbeat and breathing to slow, to the point where it is almost undetectable. It is believed that hypothermia led to declare a baby deadin Canada in 2013.

The baby in that case was born on the street in freezing cold temperatures. Doctors could not find a pulse, and the baby was declared dead. Two hours later, the baby began to move.

Dr. Michael Klein, of the University of British Columbia in Canada, said that the baby's exposure to such cold temperatures may explain the situation. "The whole circulation would have stopped but the neurological condition of the child could be protected by the cold."

Note: Many doctors refuse to admit that people going thru the Lazarus experience really died since they are brought back to life or that there was just a delay in blood flow resuming after CPR. They maintain that "calling" a death and noting the time was premature or an error in judgement. That may be the case in some situations where blood flow resumes after a few minutes, but I don't believe they have any explanation when the patient is without measurable vital signs for hours or more.

NOTE: The Lazarus Effect has even made its way into the realm of comic books. DC comics' Lazarus Pits is trending now. It deals with dead superheroes brought back to life in the DC Universe, but they come back favoring the dark side. *Came Back Wrong - What's Going On with The Lazarus Pit? Andrew Henderson Jun 1, 2022*

Taphophobia
Fear of being buried alive

"The fear of death follows from the fear of life. A man who lives fully is prepared to die at any time." —Mark Twain

The fear of being buried alive was so prevalent in the 18th and 19th centuries that the business of "Safety Coffins" became very popular. It is also the only event that I truly dread. I don't believe anything can be more horrifying than to wake up six feet under with no possible escape. That would most definitely be my final re-awakening.

In real life and even in fictional literature the subject has prevailed in the minds of humans.

"What if in the tomb I awake!" - Said Juliet in Shakespeare's Romeo and Juliet. The fearful sentiment elicits a definitive apprehension of Taphophobia, or the fear of being buried alive. That phobia was and still is very common. It was even more so in the era prior to more advanced medical practices. Some of the more famous people that suffered from that dread include Hans Christian Andersen, who asked that his veins be slit after declared dead, George Washington, Alfred Noble, and composer Fredric Chopin who forcefully dictated that his heart be removed before burial to make sure he did not come back to life in a sealed coffin. Considering past experiences, I personally have a bit of a phobia of finding myself entombed with no escape possible. I've advised my oldest grandson and granddaughter that it is my wish to be cremated after waiting a sufficient period of time. I've even said jokingly to wait until I begin to stink. I figure if Jesus raised the first Lazarus even after he began to putrify, I should not be embarrassed over a little body odor.

Fear of Being Buried Alive Phobia - Taphophobia | FEAROF

https://en.wikipedia.org/wiki/File:Wiertz_burial.jpg This work is in the public domain in the United States because it was published (or registered with the U.S. Copyright Office) before January 1, 1928.

The prevalence of diseases such as cholera and the spread of bacterial infections at a time when antibiotics and antimicrobials were not readily available or even discovered leaving many people very ill and also terrified of being prematurely declared dead. Many doctors, still, place a stethoscope above the heart and remove it in a few seconds. I believe that was the practice when doctors who attended me some 75 years ago, listened briefly and then said, "Nah, he's dead, no heartbeat, get him out of here!"

This was also the era of unreliable medical practices. Inventive ideas helped ease the minds of those terribly afraid of a too-soon burial. One clever invention was the "safety coffin." It was equipped with cotton padding for comfort, a feeding tube, a complicated arrangement of cords connected to bells and an escape hatch. Some designs ignored or forgot the need for oxygen. I did not come across any incidents where an attached bell actually rescued anyone.

Some people added requests to their wills requesting tests to verify death. These requests included pouring hot liquid on the skin and cutting them. Some wanted a crowbar and shovel, along with bells. Others were buried with fireworks and flags to let people passing by know that help was needed.

In 1791, Robert Robinson from Manchester was laid to rest in a mausoleum equipped with a unique door that the watchman could open from the outside. The coffin inside was a glass panel that could be removed. The family of the man in the casket had been told to inspect the glass for signs of condensation. If there was any evidence of breathing, he could be quickly removed. The first actual safety coffin is credited to Duke Ferdinand of Brunswick. In 1792 he was placed in a coffin with an air tube, a window to provide light, and a key in his pocket that fit the lock on the coffin lid. Now that is the kind of coffin I would want.

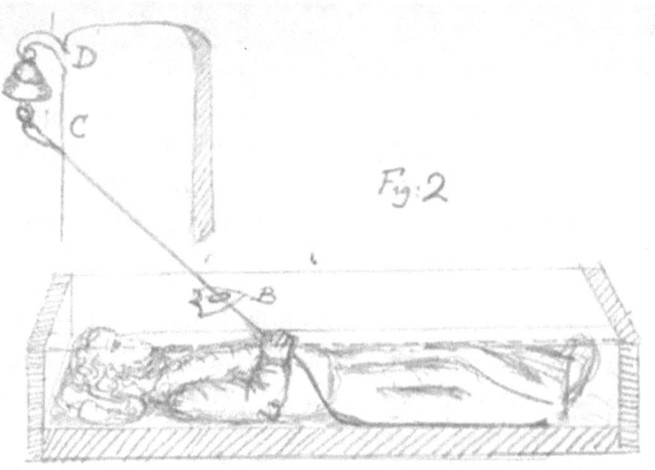

Safety Coffins could prevent people from being left to die after being buried alive. WordPress.

Tardigrade

Taking a break from death defying humans, I came across what may be the leading survivalist in the world. The creature is called a Tardigrade. I only bring this bit of information because when speaking of surviving or death-defying abilities, no one or nothing can outperform this miniscule critter.

A tiny dot sized invertebrate named by a German zoologist (Johann August Ephraim Goeze) in 1773 as "Kleiner Waasserbar" or Little Water Bear also known as a Moss Piglet. These little creatures can survive conditions that would kill humans in seconds or minutes. They can withstand extreme heat and cold, water pressure in the deepest parts of the ocean, exposure to many types of radiation and even the vacuum of space. The species has survived all 5 recorded mass extinction events. Investigations determine they've been around for over 100 million years. They also have a near exclusive talent to repair their own DNA. They can use a version of hibernation known as "tun" that can last for decades. Their life expectancy is only two to three years but can suspend its active living by entering the "tun" process and resume its existence whenever problematic conditions improve. They've been known to remain in the hibernated state for over 30 years. They are suspected to be the most resilient animal in the universe. Not sure how that claim has any evidence to back it up, since extra-terrestrial life has only been hinted at. While I do not doubt alien life forms exist, I'll wait for verification.

en.wikipedia.org/wiki/Tardigrade

Life After Death

"Our dead are never dead to us, until we have forgotten them"
—George Eliot

This is a subject in which there are many opinions. Every religious belief offers a story of the beginning of the world and humanity as well as what comes after a period of earthly existence. In reality nobody knows for sure if there is anything after one takes a last breath, and I mean a LAST breath.

I do not know either, but I can examine some of the various ideas covering the beginning and the end. Most peoples' deeply held beliefs depend on where they were born or the parents' indoctrination. True, many change their belief systems later on in life due to an epiphany, marriage, peer influence, personal research or cultish domination. Sort of like politics.

There are too many origin tales to cover here but since the main subject of the book deals with life and death, this chapter examines the different opinions of what may really happen after definitely dying,

Early humans, Neanderthals for example, began to develop a spiritual awareness and buried their dead, at times adding flowers, adornments and personal items or weapons. Cave wall paintings feature mostly hands, animals or hunts, but none offer any clues of their expectations beyond death.

When religious beliefs evolved and organized, burials and concern over post death needs became more prominent. Over the centuries rituals and entombments became more elaborate and preparing the deceased for a possible afterlife became more prominent.

Most religious beliefs offer a continuation of some form of existence after dying. The hope for eternal life and the method of achieving it is part of the sectarian indoctrination process.

Egyptians built huge pyramids to entomb their pharaohs and others of great importance. One of the first was the pyramid of Djoser in Saqqara. According to Egyptologist Salina Ikram (?), the pyramid was built about 5000 years ago and is said to be the beginning of the (Egyptian) ideas leading to re-birth and resurrection. After mummification, the deceased was placed in a sarcophagus and sealed. The walls around the sarcophagus are inscribed with thousands of hieroglyphics which are now described as spells. The incantations are for the pharaoh to use to protect him from demons and other dangerous creatures he may come across on his journey to sit with the gods. He may need to try every night for a long time until he is successful.

Although it was mainly royalty who were entombed so elaborately, it was meant to protect all the people of Egypt. The afterlife existence pf the king was required to keep the gods content and protect the living. *(1)National Geographic, The Story of God with Morgan Freeman. S1 Ep1 – Beyond Death*

Hindus' choice is to believe in re-incarnation as a way to achieve immortality. Death is just a step to another turn at living. The dead get a chance to try again after dying many times over. If the exited life was meaningful or well lived, the deceased moves on to a new life to improve his/her Karma. If the previous life was not satisfactory, the soul will also return but perhaps not as a human. The object is to achieve a certain level of perfection (some say a human has to experience all levels of existence – poverty, richness, mother, father, male, female and so on before achieving completeness. At some point, after countless lives, the soul may then end return trips to a new body and continue as a form of energy for eternity. (2) ibid

The idea that the afterlife of kings would protect and ensure energy vital for the living is also a belief held by some in Mexico, passed down from their Aztec ancestors. One day a year on "The Day of the Dead," Mexicans celebrate the lives of more recent ancestors, parents, grandparents, uncles, etc. The belief is that the divide between living and dead is not very solid. Once a year families and friends enjoy a celebration among the living to tell stories, jokes, and share meals as a way to re-connect with their departed relatives. It is one way to keep the memories alive and ensure some level of immortality for generations. (3) ibid)

One of the more popular opinions is ending up in heaven or hell. I personally object to either. I cannot accept that an all knowing, loving, compassionate deity would condemn someone to eternal damnation for committing a sin in a life lasting just a few decades. If the punishment was for a hundred, a thousand or even fifty thousand years, it would make more sense – but not forever. Imagine a child of loving parents who makes a mistake that deserves some level of punishment. The child may be punished for a period of time – no TV or phone for a week or even a month, or maybe a one-time spanking, but not every day for the rest of his life. Some chapters ago or upcoming, I mention the equally torturous "reward" of eternal heavenly bliss, so that is unacceptable also.

For Christians, the afterlife is allegedly assured due to Jesus' sacrifice or dying for everyone's sins. Since the sacrifice has been made, all believers have to do is avow they believe and they will earn eternal life. The nuances of the premise may be more complicated but that's about as simple as it can be described.

Islam offers much the same fate as Christians: Judgement – and then Heaven or Hell depending on how one behaved on Earth. There is a possible exception if the death is the result of getting killed in a Jihad in the nane Allah. The common thought is a reward of 72 Vestal Virgins in Paradise. Although the Koran does not specify a number of heavenly concubines, it does provide a description of the women.

Huda. "Islam on the Afterlife." Learn Religions, Aug. 26,
2020, learnreligions.com/islam-on-the-afterlife-2004337.

Thanatology: The Study of Death and Dying
Understanding Consciousness and Searching for the Soul

"Death is the wish of some, the relief of many, and the end of all" —Lucius Annaeus Seneca

There are more modern ideas on achieving immortality that do not include supernatural or religious beliefs or complicated rituals. Scientific methods are under study and experimentation to interfere with or reverse the death process.

Two researchers (a married couple) are conducting experiments to achieve artificial immortality. They've been married for over 30 years and would like to continue a form of relationship after death of one or the other. They have been able to create an android head into which they uploaded the memories of the wife. It is strange to watch Morgan Freeman interviewing the android head. The head responds to the name Marveena which is a combination of Marteen the husband and Veena the wife.

The couple's premise is "not to cheat death but to keep death from cheating life." They appear to want to keep at least a conscious alternative to a real living being. The head looks robotic and freely admits to being one, but the conversation is acceptably humanlike. The android's name is actually Marveena 48, which I believe refers to the 48th version or experimental attempt. Their goal in future years is to upload more than just memories with a speech pattern, but emotions and perhaps a higher level of consciousness. This method does not prevent death or prolong physical life, but it does preserve the memory in an interactive android. Aided by AI it may at least appear that the deceased will still able to interact with the living.

What is still not verifiable, is - does the talking head have any semblance of consciousness. Even if questioned and answers "yes" How would the really conscious questioner know?

A recent study, in *The Mirror* points to clues that after death, consciousness continues working after the heart stops functioning and bodily activities are no longer detectable.

Those that survived heart stoppages continued to see or sense what was happening in their surroundings even after being declared 'dead' – The awareness included observing the medical team working to revive them and listening to their comments - before their resurrection. the study suggests a person may even hear

the time of death called although while 'trapped' inside the body with some remaining brain activity.

There is a well-known doctor / researcher regarded as a leader in the field of resuscitation and consciousness.

Doctor Sam Parnia (NYU Professor of Medicine) is attempting to determine what happens after death. The studies suggest that after the body is declared to be dead, including brain death, cells throughout the body may not stop all activity the moment death occurs. Functions do not cease immediately after being officially declared dead. The doctor suspects that consciousness may continue even after the brain no longer shows signs of activity. Consciousness, the psyche, or whatever it is that makes you -you or AKA, "The Soul", he claims, is not annihilated at the moment of death. The only question is how long can it continue if the body and brain are irreversibly dead? Dr. Parnia states that it could be hours but cannot say what happens after that period of time.

Another question may be if the cells in the body and brain stay active for an extended period, can they be manipulated to re-ignite? My personal conclusion is that for some, especially those who were or remain in a cold environment, it has been true.

Dr Sam Parnia is studying consciousness after death and examining cardiac arrest cases in Europe and the US.

He said anecdotal evidence has found that people in the first phase of death may still experience some form of consciousness.

The expert. in another interview. told<u>LiveScience</u>that people who experienced cardiac arrest and suvived accurately described what was happening around them after their hearts stopped beating.

He said: "They'll describe watching doctors and nurses working, they'll describe having awareness of full conversations, of visual things that were going on, that would otherwise not be known to them."

Dr Parnia, of the NYU Langone School of Medicine in New York, said the accounts were verified by doctors and nurses, who were left stunned when informed that the patients remembered the details after being resuscitated.

His study is examining what happens to the brain after a person goes into cardiac arrest - and whether consciousness continues after death and for how long - to improve the quality of resuscitation and prevent brain injuries while restarting the heart.

Unlike the plot in Flatliners, however, when a person is resuscitated they don't return with a "magical enhancement" of their memories, said Dr Parnia.

Dr Sam Pernia, (2014-11-01) death and Consciousness–an overview of the mental and cognitive experience of death.

Another Researcher from the Medical field is also investigating Near Death Experiences and Out Of Body Events

Raymond Moody is a well-known American psychologist and medical doctor. He is best known for his research on Near-Death Experiences (NDEs) and his book "Life After Life," which was published in 1975. Chapter one in his book leads with the question: What is it like to die? I was not one of those he interviewed, but my answer to his query, would have been, "painless and uneventful" I would not have described bright lights, journey through a tunnel, receiving a joyful welcome from antecedents or the opposite – warnings to stay away from the light and to go back. As mentioned earlier, on regaining consciousness eleven days after my last search for oblivion, the first person I saw was a young ICU heart doctor. My primary interest was, "How bad was it?" He did not say a word but pantomimed chest compressions and put up two fingers, indicating twice. I smiled and told him, "Wow, two more." Months later, I requested a copy of my records. I was under critical care for eighty-five minutes, but the report did not indicate how far apart the two stoppages were. I plan to review the medical records again and try to find out.

Dr. Moody conducted extensive interviews with individuals who claimed to have had such experiences. His work has had a significant impact on the field of thanatology, which is the study of death and dying. Moody's research has helped shed light on the phenomenon of NDEs and has sparked further scientific inquiry into the nature of consciousness and the afterlife. Life After Life: The Bestselling Original Investigation That Revealed "Near-Death Experiences" *Raymond Moody MD 1975* www.lifefterlife.com

Dr. Moody, who coined the term, Near Death Experience (NDE) appears to be in search of answers to several primary questions – What is physical matter? What is consciousness? Do the two interact? Do they work side by side – need each other -? Is one primary while the other arises from it? The discussion may involve scientists, doctors, philosophers and theologists, maybe even physicists, as well as other researchers and practitioners.

During his research, he interviewed about 150 people who experienced the NDE event, He was amazed that their stories were similar in various ways even though the patients were of different religious upbringing, came from various cultures, and had varying medical histories. He also found that matching stories have been reported for thousands (?) of years and from areas all over the world. *I question the "thousands of years" part since I don't expect there to be written documentation or even less – eye witnesses.*

Until his book, Life After Life was published many doctors and lay people connected NDEs to hallucinations triggered by drugs, illegal or prescribed, lack of oxygen to the brain during the "dying" episode and even mental illness brought on by the medical condition, being treated for. That may be why many "returnees" to life were reluctant to discuss their weird stories of temporarily stepping into the other side. Today, due to the popularity and frequency of the events, there has been a marked increase in people willing to come forward with their stories. Medical personnel, relatives, and friends are less likely to ridicule their stories.

He presents two scenarios dealing with how people discuss death. One, by talking about it, many believe they are bringing it on, so they avoid the subject. Two, most languages have more words describing events and experiences acted upon, observed, and felt by their own senses and emotions while alive. Death is beyond conscious human experience. It is therefore not a common topic of discussion and since most have not been through it previously, there are fewer words to describe the event. (I believe I would have the words, if only I had the memory.) Other factors are social taboos and the fatalistic event itself may be too fearful to merit discussion. *Life After Life: The Bestselling Original Investigation That Revealed "Near-Death Experiences" Raymond Moody MD 1975*

The two MDs cited, study death and dying but with slightly different primary practices although with similar objectives. Doctor Parnia was a critical care physician but presently is more involved in determining how long the "soul" remains in or near the body, how long it can continue, does it dissipate into the ether, or does it travel somewhere else?

Dr. Moody is a practicing psychologist who is also more interested in the journey of life's essence or the "soul".

NDEs and OBEs

"Many people die at twenty five and aren't buried until they are seventy five" —Benjamin Franklin

The following are six stories by people who recall Out of Body Experiences. The names of the individuals are apparently pseudonyms. I did not alter their narratives and are direct quotes as reported by The Mirror <u>What comes after death? 6 people who've come back from the grave reveal what happens when we die - Mirror Online</u>

1-Like reading a book

Five years ago *monitormonkey* underwent major surgery during which he bled out, causing him to die for several minutes, <u>The Mirror</u>reported.

"I woke up in what looked like space but there weren't any stars or light. I wasn't floating so to speak, I was just there.

"I wasn't hot or cold, hungry or tired - just a peaceful neutral kind of thing. I knew there was light and love somewhere nearby but I had no urge or need to go to it right away.

"I remember thinking over my life, but it wasn't like a montage. More like I was idly flipping through a book and snippets stood out here and there.

"Whatever it was, it changed my thoughts on a few things. I am still afraid to die, but I'm not worried about what happens after that."

2-A visit from someone dear

Schneidah7 was thrown from his motorbike while cruising at 50mph and was medically dead when he was taken to hospital. As he lay in the road before the ambulance came, he recalled someone he knew encouraging him.

"I just remember being on the pavement and things slowly going black and quiet.

"The only reason I didn't fall asleep was because of a bizarre moment where I heard someone yelling, 'Ranger up you candy f***! Come on man, get up. Get up. GET UP!'

"Then someone was slapping my helmet (which was basically smushed really hard onto my head).

"When I opened my eyes I saw my brother squatting on the pavement next me to. This was odd because my brother died from an overdose several years ago.

"The only other thing I remember is him glancing at his watch and saying something like 'They'll be here soon' and then walking away.

"I wish I could give more detail but I honestly don't remember much of the incident and still have trouble with my memory as a result of the accident."

While many users described their 'death' as being like a void, IDiedForABit had a very different experience after an allergic reaction caused his or her heart to stop.

"I remember a feeling of being sucked backwards, extremely slowly, like being pulled through water and this blackness fading in and out.

"At one point it faded back in and I was staring out at a garden.

"It wasn't filled with flowers, just dust and patchy grass. There was a playground with a merry-go-round in the middle and two children running around it. A boy and a girl.

"It's difficult to describe but I got the feeling I could choose if I wanted to stay or leave, but every time I tried to go back I was held in place.

"I went through all the reasons I wanted to go back, and when I told the presence I didn't want to abandon my mother whatever held me finally let go.

"I snapped back into my body. My heart had stopped for six minutes."

3-A garden

While many users described their 'death' as being like a void, IDiedForABit had a very different experience after an allergic reaction caused his or her heart to stop.

"I remember a feeling of being sucked backwards, extremely slowly, like being pulled through water and this blackness fading in and out.

"At one point it faded back in and I was staring out at a garden.

"It wasn't filled with flowers, just dust and patchy grass. There was a playground with a merry-go-round in the middle and two children running around it. A boy and a girl.

"It's difficult to describe but I got the feeling I could choose if I wanted to stay or leave, but every time I tried to go back I was held in place.

"I went through all the reasons I wanted to go back, and when I told the presence I didn't want to abandon my mother whatever held me finally let go.

"I snapped back into my body. My heart had stopped for six minutes."

4 -Hitting snooze

As a teenager, *TheDeadManWalks* had been going through months of chemotherapy when his nose started bleeding uncontrollably.

Due to a sepsis and *Clostridium difficile* infection, his condition worsened, and he slipped in and out of death, which he describes beautifully.

"The worst part of it all, looking back, is how peaceful it can seem.

"It's like wanting to hit the snooze button on your alarm at 7am.

"And maybe you do hit it once or twice but then you remember that you have work or school and that sleep can wait because you've still got s*** to do."

5-Or is it a laugh?

altburger69's brush with death didn't stop them from cracking jokes. "Had a heart attack last year and my heart stopped three times in the emergency room. "Apparently, each time they shocked me back I 'woke up' (how it felt) and told the staff a different knock-knock joke each time."No lights or whatever, just felt like sleep."

6-There is nothing after

In the aftermath of a motorbike accident, *Rullknuf's* breathing and pulse stopped and he went "cramp and stiff". After two minutes, his friend managed to resuscitate him.

"For me it was just a blackout. No dreams, no visions, just nothing.

"Apparently I asked over 10 times what happened and said I shall be happy to be alive today."

> Six people who 'came back from the dead' reveal what really happens when you die - CoventryLive (coventrytelegraph.net) What comes after death? 6 people who've come back from the grave reveal what happens when we die - Mirror Online

Seeking Immortality

"How can the dead be truly dead when they still live in the souls of those who are left behind?"—Carson McCullers

I have mentioned the erection of pyramids to safeguard the mummified remains of Egyptian kings and queens, the construction of android heads and androids to safekeep memories and emotions, freezing heads and bodies in the hope of future restoration to active live, the study of consciousness' composition and survival – perhaps in the hope of bottling it up until a host body can be constructed or cloned, Artificial Intelligence implanted chips to overcome human ailments and disabilities to prolong lives, and yet to be discovered even more amazing innovations.

There is a simpler way to achieve a level of immortality. Others have done it and many more will do it in the future. I am doing it now. It was first done about 3000 years ago by Rameses the 3ʳᵈ of Egypt. In the city of Thebes, now known as Luxor, he constructed the Temple of a Million Years. It is not a tomb but a memorial mortuary where people can visit to invoke his spirit and read about his exploits, It is actually a huge biographical construct. The words and symbols depicting the Pharoah's life and accomplishments were etched deep into the stone so that they could not be erased by humans or nature. The feeling was that anytime someone mentioned his name. his life was renewed, and he would therefore live eternally in others' memories.

I said others have done it and many more will, including me. I do not mean build memorial temples but write biographies and memoirs. Talk to your children and grandchildren, especially about ancestors you remember. Even better, those that left written documents, photographs, videos. and other memorabilia.

American Presidential Libraries appear to serve the same purpose, except that they are not considered mausoleums or temples.

There is always the chance that one or more of my writings will become popular enough to exist for a few years after I depart. If not royalties, I can leave my descendants a few memories. At the very least I can be an entry in GOOGLE search.

Artificial Intelligence

"If being a kid is about learning how to live, then being a grown-up is about learning how to die" —Stephen King

On a curious whim, after reading various articles on AI or Artificial Intelligence, I tried asking the AI unit featured on **ChatAI.com** to determine what opinion, if any, it might present on the subject of life after death. I include the answers here because they more or less agree with other research. I also asked about Near Death Experience and about AI's possible contribution to prolonging human life.

One version of AI answered with:

"Hello! When it comes to theories of life after death, there are various beliefs and ideas. Three of the most commonly discussed theories are:

1. Reincarnation: This theory suggests that after death, a person's soul is reborn into a new body. The specific form of the new life may depend on one's actions and karma in the previous life. Reincarnation is a concept found in many religions, such as Hinduism and Buddhism.

2. Spiritual Existence: This theory proposes that after death, the soul or consciousness continues to exist in a spiritual realm. It suggests that individuals may experience an afterlife that is separate from the physical world. Different religions and spiritual traditions have their own interpretations of what this afterlife might be like.

3. Eternal Oblivion: This theory posits that after death, there is simply nothingness. It suggests that consciousness ceases to exist, and there is no continuation of life or afterlife. This perspective is often associated with atheism or agnosticism, where the belief in a higher power or an afterlife is absent.

It's important to note that these theories are based on beliefs and philosophical perspectives, and there is no scientific consensus on what happens after death. Different cultures and individuals may have their own unique theories and interpretations as well."

(On AI future use/capabilities)

"AI Can certainly play a role in researching and developing methods to prevent death or extend life. AI technologies can be used in medical research, drug discovery and personalized healthcare, among other areas to advance our understanding of aging and improve our ability to treat diseases. However. it's important to note that the concept of life after death is a philosophical and religious question that goes beyond the scope of AI's capabilities.

Near death experiences are subjective experiences reported by individuals who have come close to death or have been clinically dead and then revived. While these experiences are real in the sense that people genuinely report having them, the interpretation of these experiences varies. Some believe that near death experiences provide evidence of an afterlife or spiritual realm, while others attribute them to physiological and psychological factors. The scientific community is still studying and researching near death experiences to better understand their nature and significance." ***ChatAI.com 2023***

 Similar to human assumptions, beliefs, or theories, even AI programs do not completely agree and offered answers that were slightly different.

Another AI program included the spiritual version as Number three and disregarded the Eternal Oblivion fate:

"Determining the highest possibility of truth for theories of life after death is subjective and depends on individual beliefs and perspectives. However, I can provide you with three commonly discussed theories that have gained some traction among different cultures and religions. These theories are:

1. Reincarnation: This theory suggests that after death, an individual's soul is reborn into a new body. The specific

circumstances of the new life are believed to be influenced by the actions and choices made in previous lives. Reincarnation is a central concept in Hinduism, Buddhism, and some other belief systems.

2. Heaven and Hell: This theory posits that after death, individuals are rewarded or punished based on their actions and beliefs during their lifetime. Those who have lived virtuously and followed religious teachings may go to a heavenly realm, while those who have committed evil deeds may be condemned to a place of punishment or suffering. This theory is prominent in many religious traditions, including Christianity and Islam.

3. Spiritual Existence: This theory suggests that after death, the soul or consciousness continues to exist in a non-physical form. It may involve concepts such as becoming one with a universal consciousness, merging with a divine entity, or simply existing as a disembodied spirit. This theory is found in various spiritual and philosophical traditions It's important to note that these theories are based on faith, personal beliefs, and cultural traditions rather than scientific evidence. It remains a mystery, and different individuals may have different interpretations and beliefs." ***AI at AWS 2023***

Obviously, Artificial Intelligence can also have different ideas concerning the hereafter if any exists. It is also not shy in admitting that it can be mystified by seeming unanswerable queries.

The information provided by AI does not cite sources. I believe it searches ala Google and chooses the most popular and preferred answers to the questions posed. Most of the answers given agree, more or less, with my own research.

Death After Life

"I'm the one that's got to die when it's time for me to die, so let me live my life the way I want to." —Jimi Hendrix

The majority of this book has dealt with the process of death, resurrection and comments on after life possibilities, Most of those resuscitated were glad to have a second chance (and more than one opportunity for a few others), while some may have preferred to remain dead. There are many alive today who have not gone through the process of reviving but are hoping for an end to their current miserable condition in life. There are countless individuals who are totally paralyzed, are in constant pain, have other disabilities that prevent a functional life. Plus the scourge of diseases with no available remedies or hope for improvement. Add to that group the unfortunates with dementia with little or no awareness of even being alive. Who would undoubtedly, if given the choice, would opt to release a family caretaker from the burden of caring for a person with disabilities.

AI

Society, religious groups, and the law itself frown upon or disallow freedom of choice when death would be the the preferred option. People that would opt for a quick end if they had the ability or the means are sentenced to a life of permanent disability, stress, discomfort, and at times, sheer agony. Sometimes the agony is suffered by family members who have to care for the incapacitated patients.

Researchers such as AI developers, medical pioneers, and individuals such as Elon Musk are looking for ways to restore physical and mental abilities, and most important, quality of life, to those with limited or lost functions.

Elon Musk has invested in producing a mental implant developed to help paraplegics and other disabled regain use of legs, arms, and other physical abilities. Including sight. The implant (Neuralink) in the brain is designed to form a symbiotic connection between the brain and Artificial Intelligence. The coin sized chip is imbedded in the skull, tiny wires about 20 times thinner than a strand of hair spread out through the brain. The wires are so thin that a human surgeon cannot perform the surgery. To overcome that dilemma Musk's laboratories developed a robotic surgeon to handle the task. The machine surgeon is about eight feet tall. The robot is more dexterous than a human and is equipped with a needle that adjusts automatically to the motions of the subject brain caused by breathing and even heartbeats. Andrew Hires, a neurologist at the University of Southern California

Elon Musk's company is called Neuralink. It is designed to create a symbiotic connection between the brain and the brain and Artificial intelligence. Musk refers to it as "FitBit for your skull."

The company's objective is to: "Create a generalized brain interface to restore autonomy to those with unmet medical needs today and unlock human potential tomorrow.

To restore independence and improve lives, we've built a brain-computer interface (BCI) experience that enables fast and reliable computer control and prioritizes ease of use."

Neuralink

Technological improvements in Neuralink can assist in treating Alzheimer's and other neurological problems. Professor Andrew Hires also said other applications might allow people to control robotic prostheses with their minds.

"The first application you can imagine is better mental control for a robotic arm for someone who's paralyzed," *Dr. Andrew Hires Insider 2019* Dr. Hires added that brain implanted electrodes could help reproduce the sense of touch giving the user finer control using a prosthetic device.

"The first indication this device is intended for is to help quadriplegics regain their digital freedom by allowing users to interact with their computers or phones in a high bandwidth and naturalistic way. The funds from the round will be used to take Neuralink's first product to market and accelerate the research and development of future products," Neuralink said in a blog post. Series C Funding Round Announcement | Blog | Neuralink

There are several YouTube episodes highlighting the development, use and progress of the Neuralink brain implant. The videos are full of information. I was more interested in how the implanted chip works. The basic premise is that

paralysis or loss of use sets in when a signal sent from the brain to an arm, leg or any other body part is interrupted due to trauma or any other factor. The intended target cannot receive the signal. The Neuralink device is able to duplicate the function of neurons and can deliver the brain signals that were previously interrupted. Signals sent are wireless. The potential to remedy multiple conditions is incredible. Among the list are hearing, sight, paralysis, addiction, anxiety, and various neurological disorders. In an MSNBC program a representative from ant AI proponents suggested that the wireless method could lead to hackers taking over a person's movements or actions or controlling their minds. This led me to suggest that AI should be programmed with Isaac Asimov's factionary, but doable Three Laws of Robotics

One of the YouTube presentations suggested that a user can even use it to summon his/her Tesla telepathically. As I write this, it is Christmas Eve 2023 and I'm finishing up the gift wrapping. I was listening to Elon Musk and some of his expert advisors and employees. While wrapping. I heard some amazing plans and predictions of what Neuralink will be capable of doing not too far in the future. One of the most encouraging expectations is a secondary implant that will receive the signal from the brain implant while bypassing the injured body part that was preventing delivery of the brain's command. A compromised spinal cord will not hinder the effect of the Neuralink chips. Another fascinating possibility is that even if parts of the eyes are damaged, it may still be able to restore sight.

In addition, at The Wall Street Journal CEO Council Summit in December 2021, Musk said the first humans into whom Neuralink hopes to implant its devices are people who: "have severe spinal cord injuries like tetraplegics, quadriplegics."

Elon Musk also says that in the long term, Neuralink's chip could be used to meld human consciousness with artificial intelligence — though experts are skeptical of this. Despite doubts among some technological and neurological authorities. It is usually individuals with a vision that strive to do what others believe difficult and even impossible. *Elon Musk Neuralink Presentation on YouTube*

It is encouraging that there is ongoing medical research to help those that need the most help, especially those that have lost critical bodily functions with good years remaining to enjoy life. Among them. children, young adults, and veterans who were injured while serving the country.

My concern centers around the possibility that AI, especially when installed in humanoid robots or androids may continue to evolve and endanger humanity. Isaac Asimov in his Robot novels suggested that the safe guard of "The Three Laws of Robotics" must be part of the technological programming. The three laws are:

> "The First Law: A robot may not injure a human being or,
> through inaction, allow a human being to come to harm.
> The Second Law: A robot must obey the orders given it
> by human beings except where such orders would conflict
> with the First Law.
> The Third Law: A robot must protect its own existence as
> long as such protection does not conflict with the First or
> Second Law."- Isaac Asimov <u>Three Laws of Robotics -
> Wikipedia</u>

I went right to the source and asked ChatAI if any developers were considering adding the 3 laws of robotics into AI programming. Surprisingly the answer was in the affirmative, but the laws need to be modified or expanded to manage the complexities of AI systems, and the implementation is still in debate.

Gene Editing

*Death has been stalking me since the day I was born… but it
does not appear to be in a rush."*—J. Reyes

Another medical treatment that could be promising is gene therapy
including gene addition and gene editing. There are several methods of
gene editing. Among them are

ZFNs (zinc finger nucleases)
Talens (transcription activator-like-effector nucleases)
CRISPR (clustered regularly interspaced short
palindromic repeats)

I have a very basic and minimal understanding of the process of
gene editing, but scientists have a very weird method of naming and
explaining procedures or treatments that make them undecipherable.
I've never heard of the first two on the list. I did (laboriously) read a book
on CRISPR but only understood a very few elements of the process.
Relying on memory only, the basic idea is to find a defective gene using
RNA that is programmed to search, then deliver a tool like messenger
(an enzyme) to cut out or turn off the defective gene. It is possible but
more difficult to insert a replacement gene. One of the important uses
of gene editing is to edit pig organ DNA to make it more acceptable in
a human host, lessening the risk of organ rejection.

That's about as basic as I remember. I don't know anything about the
first two. Number three looks promising and there is a lot of interest in
perfecting the process of altering the human genome. I must confess
that curiosity got the best of me, and I had to verify if my memory
was accurate. That's the benefit of the internet – knowledge is at your
fingertips. My memory was okay but a little behind the times – in just
this last year progress has blossomed.

In one year, dozens of research papers have been presented to tout the results of studies using CRISPR to cut out defective DNA and replace it. Using the method to treat cancer, HIV, blindness, chronic pain, muscular dystrophy and more. It was also used for sickle cell anemia and hemophilia.

10 Amazing Things Scientists Just Did withCRISPR www.livescience.com/59602-crispr-advances-gene-editing-field.html

A lot of these developments are coming in a little too late for me with my host of ailments and also for my brother who is now blind. But at the current rate of progress my grandkids and great-grandkids are still young enough to enjoy the benefits being developed. It would certainly help if any of my books became best sellers, and I could leave them the means to afford treatments if or when needed.

Parte 2

MEMOIR

Moving on with life
Close Calls
Military
Vietnam
Agent Orange
Business
Law Enforcement
Higher Education
Retirement
Footnotes

Moving On With Life After youthful deaths.

"Everybody is going to be dead one day, just give them time."
—Neil Gaiman,

After my last infantile encounter with premature death, great changes were on the horizon. My mother's vow still had a couple of years of tenure left. Here I was, a boy with pigtails wearing a dress (an ugly one at that) andinfinitely embarrassed. Ibloodied many a nose and lips defending my dignity dealing with insensitive school bullies. Since my fighting skills and physique did not match my rage nor did the mane of hair give me Samson like strength, I bled more than a few times myself.

Sometimes, when strangers, usually women,praised me with, "*Hay que nena linda.*" ("Oh, what a cute little girl") I would angrily respond by lifting the damn robe, exposing myself and screaming, "Soy nene!"(I'm a boy!) By the way, when I became a little more sentient, I insisted on wearing pants under the habit. Years later, Johnny Cash's song, "A Boy Named Sue" became one of my favorites since it reminded me of what I went through as a boy wearing long hair and a tasseled frock. That was long before long hair was fashionable or acceptable for men and boys. The long awaited for the shearing of my locks finally arrived. It was my first haircut in many years and at the time, the happiest day of my life/

The pigtails were cut but kept their braided style. The anniversary of the Virgin of Monserrate's appearance was coming and the vow had to be completed by laying the sheared locks at the idol's feet. The harrowing ritual's final phase was to climb a tall hill where the altar had been built. The hundreds of worshippers who had completed their penitence were required to climb the hill *on their knees,* braving the rocks, weeds, twigs, bugs and whatever else littered the path. Even though I was not the one who initiated the vow, I was bound by my mother's oath to join her up the hill on my knees. My mother was not abusive but her beliefs and the church's edicts and rituals overcame laws and common sense. In the end, The trek was worth the effort. My tresses would never haunt me again. They were abandoned at the feet of a lifeless alabaster statue never to distress me again.

My father and I (wearing the habit)
My long hair in pigtails behind my back

"If death meant just leaving the stage long enough to change costume and come back as a new character. Would you slow down? Or speed up?" –Chuck Palahniuk

In a few years' time, nature worked its magic and turned the sickly often dying boy into a healthy pre-teen. It was a rebirth but more like a caterpillar reborn as a butterfly. He morphed from a thin Friar Tuck-looking monk into a healthy, handsome junior James Bond escorting the princess at the king's ball. Or, in this case, the daughter of the richest family in town.

Soon after this celebration honoring my hometown's patron saint, my parents made plans to migrate to the US mainland. I wondered why they wanted to make such a drastic move but neither my brother nor I were old enough to voice an opinion unfavorable to their decision. We were doing quite well as it was. My father was an auto mechanic making a good living and earning extra by buying used bicycles and converting them into an early version of mopeds. He was an inventor as well as a multi-talented handyman. Our home was near the beach, so he built it with the back part mounted on stilts and a workshop underneath. My mother had no need to work. My brother and I were doing very well in school, thanks to her early tutoring. The school selected my brother to attend a school for gifted students, but my mother did not allow it due to his young age and the distance to the new advanced school.

Our backyard was the ocean, and the front yard a lush, wooded hill for a playground. My mother had heard the rumors suggesting the "streets paved with gold" rumors and convinced my father that we would be better off on the US mainland. They did plan the move well, though. My mother would move first, get a job while my father remained on the island and sell our house. My first question when arriving in Philadelphia was, "Donde esta la playa?" *(Where's the beach?)* I was heartbroken when my mother said there was none.

When my mother left, my father had said that he would not go until he had a job waiting. That's exactly what he did. He arrived on a Saturday and went to his new job the very next Monday morning. I've always wondered how he accomplished that. This was long before e-mail, cell phones, and texting. It was all done via snail mail and long-distance phone calls. Another obstacle he somehow overcame was that he did not speak a word of English, was not familiar with the new city, nor how to get around. Yet he made it to work the first day. His first assignment was to install snowplows on jeeps and pickup trucks. He had never seen snow nor snowplows before in his life, but unfamiliarity with the equipment did not deter him.

He had a long successful run on his first job plus he rented a garage where he worked for himself in the evenings and weekends to earn a little extra.

For my brother and me, learning the new language was fairly easy at our age, but I, for one had a rough start.

My first day in school, the teacher said something to the class, but I had no clue what she was saying so I did nothing. She came closer to me and kept repeating the words louder and louder. I was near tears when she turned to her desk, pulled out a thick ruler and started beating my hands and yelling the same phrase. One kid yelled, "He doesn't speak English!" Someone found a way to explain what it meant- the phrase was "Fold your hands." That was the first English phrase I learned. For those not of that era, it was customary to fold your hands while the teacher was speaking to the class. Teachers were also free to use rulers and paddles as corporal punishment.

A few days later, I needed to go to the bathroom, so I did what most schoolkids in the world do, I raised my hand. I stood and told her in Spanish. Of course, she did not understand. This time, she sent one of my classmates to another room to get someone who spoke Spanish. This was in 1953, there were not too many Latinos in our neighborhood yet.

A girl who spoke Spanish arrived and asked what I wanted. I told her and she turned to the teacher and said, "He has to pee." The laughter that followed was raucous and at that instant I realized that I had to learn the new language as fast as possible. My brother and I helped each other by practicing and teaching each other any new words we learned. We also found some shortcuts. We discovered that any English word ending in "tion" was the same word and had the same meaning in Spanish when the "t" was replaced with a "c." There are exceptions, but very few. The same works in reverse. There are approximately 13,000 English words that become Spanish just by changing the "t" to a "c"- "information" becomes "informacion" with a slight change in pronunciation.

Our mother helped by buying us comic books, and other children's books and later Encyclopedia Brittanica. Another helpful hint was making sure we watched news programs since she knew that broadcasters had excellent grammar and pronunciation. In a few short months we were both "A" students.

Life continued about as normal as that of any pre-teen or teenager except for the incidents described in the next chapter - Close Calls.

CLOSE CALLS

"What do we say to the Lord of Death? 'Not today."
—George R.R. Martin

The following situations did not cause death but some certainly would have, had not whatever it is that protects me was present.

Age 9 – Coney Island, NY. On a trip to Coney Island amusement park, I wanted to get on the Roller Coaster. This one was called The Cyclone. I boarded with my aunt who was a whole lot more rotund than I was. The safety belt secured her tightly but was very loose around me. At its biggest drop of 85 feet on a steep descent angle and a speed of about 60 miles per hour, the car went down but my unsecured skinny body went up. My aunt reacted instantly and grabbed my legs before I flew out of the car. She squeezed me until the ride was over. She cried, I didn't. It was an exhilarating ride. On future rides, though, I made sure I was securely fastened.

Age 14 – Went to a neighborhood pool with my brother, an uncle, and other friends. My uncle did not know how to swim. He fell into the deep end of the pool. I saw that he was in distress, I yelled for my brother who was at the far end of the pool. I dove in, hoping to hold his head up above water until my brother or other help arrived. My plan worked for a few seconds, but my uncle panicked, reached down, grabbed my head and put his legs around me. We sank and both would have drowned had not help arrived. My brother had run to the deep end of the pool dove in and forcefully yanked our uncle off me. I was then able to surface and breathe again. I watched as my brother pushed my uncle to the edge of the pool. Others then lifted him out of the water.

Age 15 Thomas Edison HS Philadelphia. I was in my first week or so of High School. Walking in the hallway en route to a class, a much bigger boy than I bumped into me. I thought nothing of it and kept on walking. He was with three friends. He yelled at me, "Hey kid, aren't you going to say excuse me?" The cockiness in me did not consider the consequences, so I said, "Why? You bumped into me."

He then said, "Nah, that's not how it goes. We gotta settle this."

I thought to myself that I was in deep trouble; four against one. But I've never backed down and have always been too cocky for my size. In that era, disputes were settled by going to the boys' lavatory and duking it out. So, the four of them and I headed to the nearest bathroom. Once in the room he took off his jacket and started dancing around as if he were Muhammad Ali. I put my books on the floor and just stood there. All of a sudden, the door slammed open and three giant boys stormed in. I'm thinking to myself, "Oh damn, I'm in deeper trouble now." The biggest boy stood right in front of me, grabbed my chin in his giant hand and moved it side to side.

He then asked, "You Caveman's brother?"

With hidden glee, I said, "Yeah! yeah!"

He then turned to my would-be assailant, grabbed him by his shirt, banged him against the wall, and said, "You don't mess with Caveman's brother!" (Although he did not say "mess.")

He let him go and the four aggressors ran out of the bathroom.

My brother's nickname is Caveman, he is bigger than I am and played on the High School football team with the three giants that saved me, at least from a severe beating. No one ever challenged me again. Every once in a while, I would walk the school halls flanked by two or more huge football players.

 Age 15 – During a Boy Scout Jamboree I participated in a tumbling exhibition and landed on my head instead of gracefully on my feet. The blow knocked me out and dropped my blood pressure to near zero. I ended up in a coma for three days. When discharged from the hospital, I was under the impression that I had fully recovered but a few months later I discovered that a chunk of my memory was gone. The accident happened during the summer vacation the year I was to begin High School in September.

In one of the early days of the new school year, I was waiting outside the gym for the previous class to come out and my class to enter. The class started to come out, but one boy stopped suddenly called my name and in apparent joy quickly moved closer to greet me, I was surprised and stepped back. I did not know who he was. He looked hurt or disappointed at the way I reacted. He told me his name and that we were friends when he lived in my neighborhood, but his family moved to another area during the past summer.

I told him, "Look, I don't know who you are." He then told me that his mother was picking him up at the 7th street entrance after school and asked me to meet him there so his mother could prove we were friends. Reluctantly and out of sheer curiosity, I agreed and met him after school. His mother was also a complete stranger though she seemed overjoyed at seeing me and talked to me as if I were a family member. She asked about my parents and my brother, all by name. I told her, "I'm sorry ma'am, I don't remember any of you." We parted ways with all involved perplexed and somewhat disappointed.

When I got home, I told my mother the story and told her the mother's name. Again, a look of surprise and glee from her and asked me how I could forget a kid that was one of my best friends and the family that lived right across the street. I'm not sure if I avoided him or he avoided me from then on, but we never made contact again that year or any other. I've considered trying hypnosis to see if that memory can be restored.

To this day, the mystery continues. I still don't remember the boy nor anyone in his family. I believe that the trauma to my skull caused selective amnesia if there is such a term or condition.

Age 17 – Downtown Philadelphia. Crossing a street on a green light, I heard a screech, turned to my left, and got hit by a car. The impact sent me flying but received only scratches, bruises, and a painful knee…no breaks, no blood. The doctor suggested I sue, but I had no significant injury.

Age 22 – Philadelphia, working at my gas station, a convertible with 5 men in the car pulled up to the pump and ordered $5 of gas. At twenty-two cents a gallon, it was a nice order. I began to pump the gas and all the men came out of the car. They positioned themselves behind me. One pulled a gun and pointed it at me. As usual, I did not panic but in reality, felt helpless. My trained German Shepherd came out to stand beside me and I whispered the signal "watch em" which just means to bark and growl but not attack. The dog began to bark and growl. I finished pumping at about the same time. The men, apparently in fear of my defender, jumped in their car, threw a five-dollar bill in the air and drove off. As an afterthought, I did not believe they planned to rob me or hurt me; I'll never know for sure if it was just a practical joke, but without certainty of their intentions, I've included it as a close call. I was also extremely proud of and grateful for my canine savior. Other than my days in 'Nam, that was my first encounter with an armed opponent as a civilian. There were more to come in my future.

Age 23- Philadelphia - Driving a recently souped up '57 Chevy, I ran a stop sign and was struck by a brand-new Mercedes. The impact forced ne to slide across the bench seat (seat belts were not legally required at the time). I broke the passenger window with my head and then broke the windshield with my skull when the car struck the front steps of the corner property. The police drove me to the nearest hospital where I was treated for bruises and released. My friend picked me up at the hospital and we drove to the scene to check on my car. My car was totaled, and we were both amazed that I survived with just a headache and some bruises.

Age 28 - Long Island, NJ Went on a SCUBA diving trip with my cousin to explore a sunken ship off Long Island in South Jersey. My cousin entered the ship through a hole in the hull but became tangled in some hanging wires. I saw he was struggling and approached his position. Underwater divers can communicate only with hand signals. I sensed that he was beginning to panic. I would be unable to cut the metal cables with my diving knife. I had to calm him down and maneuver him out of the tangle of wires in the opposite direction he went in. In other words, back him out. It took an excruciating few minutes to complete the extraction. He calmed down as soon as he was free, and we surfaced safely. Had he panicked and grabbed me, we both would have been entangled in the wires, run out of oxygen, and drowned.

Age 32- This is the strangest and most inexplicable event of my life. I need an answer to solve the mystery but I'm loath to visit a medium or psychic to seek help. I will consider any theories.

On I-95 somewhere in North Carolina en route to Florida, a trip that I made and still do frequently. Cruising along at the then posted speed of 60MPH, I suddenly became very nervous and began to shake. I felt an overwhelming need to stop. I am not psychic nor a believer in the supernatural. Yet that one time I just knew I had to obey the extremely forceful urge that I had to stop. There were no ghostly voices, dark premonitions or any other warning except my body's physical, unnatural nervous spasms I pulled over to the right shoulder and shut off the car engine. About 10 minutes later. I heard and saw a fleet of police, fire and rescue vehicles fly by where I was parked.

By then, the nervousness and anxiety had dissipated. Feeling calm and with no sense of dread, I started the engine and pulled out onto the highway. Ten miles down the road I came across an impressive sight. A tractor trailer that had been heading north veered across the median, crossed over to the south bound side, flipped over, lost its cargo of what appeared to be telephone poles and ended in the woods off the south bound lanes. The highway was littered with telephone poles and blocked by first responder vehicles, so I had to pull over again to wait for the accident scene to be cleared. I watched as Fire rescue used special equipment to remove the truck driver who was trapped in the cab. I began to do some quick math and concluded that had I continued at 60 miles an hour for the previous ten minutes when I forced myself to stop, I would have been at the very spot I was now and would have been on the receiving end of an out-of-control truck and scores of flying telephone poles. I have never had any premonitions before nor after that incident. It is totally unexplainable, but it happened, and I will never forget it. Readers should know by now that I am a non-believer of any supernatural creatures, deities, demons, saints, guardian angels or any other religious or superstitious elements. It was a non-specific premonition that served me well that night. Most of my family members who follow religious beliefs insist that I am here for a reason. If so, whatever it is I'm supposed to do, I have not done it yet and I'm running out of time.

Age 35 – Philadelphia Office of the Sheriff. Transporting a prisoner to the hospital and driving through a housing project, a shot rang out. My partner stopped the van, and I stepped out of the van. As I got out, a young man ran across the street in my direction and crashed into my van. I looked down and saw a spot of blood on his right buttock, I drew my gun when I saw an older man about 15 feet away on the curb across from me with a gun in his hand. He was surrounded by a crowd of spectators. I could not shoot for fear of collateral damage. The armed man apparently had not noticed me or my marked vehicle. His attention was focused on his primary target, but when he saw me, said "Oh shit! He put his gun in a black bag and ran off. He was dressed in all black and jumped into a white Caddy. I could not give chase because I had a sick inmate in the van and a bleeding victim at my side. When the kid turned to face me, the front of his pants was soaked in blood. Backup arrived in minutes. I gave them the description of the shooter and the car.

The gunman was apprehended by the police shortly after. The young man was transported in a police car but died on the way to the hospital.

For those who wonder why I did not shoot – I am, (or was), an expert marksman but that was in an indoor range and a controlled environment, in a secure setting shooting at paper targets that do not shoot back, where there is no excessive adrenalin flowing, no crowd of spectators, where there were no gusts of wind, and plenty time to take a deep breath, aim carefully, and squeeeeze the trigger. Only the Lone Ranger shot the gun out of a villain's hand in every TV episode without even taking time to aim or spilling a drop of blood.

In later years when mass shootings became frequent events, I wrote several newspaper articles denouncing the idea proposed by ill-informed politicians of arming teachers in schools. The main argument against that practice is that a "gun in hand" is many times more effective than a gun in holster, in a purse, in a pocket, a desk drawer or a closet. When a determined shooter walks into a room all he needs to do is pull the trigger. The teacher may have a gun somewhere in the room but not readily available; nor will said teacher have the experience, training or mind set to use the weapon properly.

Age 37 – I-95 Philadelphia - On my motorcycle with my young son in the back seat, my rear tire suffered a blowout. The bike swayed from lane to lane while I tried to slow it down and stop. Lucky for us that traffic on I-95 that day was light and the cars behind me, realizing my predicament, slowed down to give me room to maneuver the disabled bike to a safe stop on the right shoulder. Some drivers yelled "good job" as they passed by. My son never rode with me again. That was one of the events that gave me a clue that those in my vicinity are also safer when things go wrong.

An accident on a motorcycle is more often fatal for both driver and passenger.

Age 38 – Leaving work in my new Pontiac Trans-Am, a pick-up truck ran a light and broadsided my car on the passenger side. My vehicle was wrecked beyond repair. I walked away without a scratch. Just upset that my new car was destroyed.

Age 42- Office of the Sheriff While conducting an eviction, I made the mistake of not waiting for my partner. I had done many evictions with no problems and became complacent. I knocked on the door to serve notice. An older man opened the door and pointed a shotgun right to my face. He then said, "You ain't taking ma house." My Glock was in my holster; but that is not much good there. I have previously mentioned, a "gun in hand" is a thousand times better than a gun in holster. Again, I did not panic. I simply put my hands in front of me and said, "Sorry sir, didn't mean to upset you." and very slowly walked back to a safer distance. I then called for backup and a SWAT unit, managed the situation without firing a shot. The man was arrested, and we repossessed his property.

Age 44- Just a few years after totaling my second car, I was cruising along on 5th Street in Philadelphia, crossing Allegheny Avenue when a limousine struck my car's driver's side quarter panel at about 60 miles per hour. My car did a complete 180-degree spin. Three cars totaled that ended up in a junkyard but again, I walked away unharmed. A crowd of people surrounded the limousine while my car and I were totally ignored. I found out later that the limo passenger was the famous WWE professional wrestler, Shawn Michaels.

Age 52 Cruising at 42,000 feet over the Atlantic Ocean. On a vacation trip to the Caribbean, the plane I was in, accompanied by my parents and some of my grandkids, was struck by lightning. The interior lights went out, the plane shuddered and dropped what seemed to be about a thousand feet.

The panic and the screamed pleas for divine intervention of the 150 plus passengers are difficult to describe.

As I may have mentioned several times, I do not panic easily. I am a firm believer that worry, complaints, and panic serve no useful purpose. Many people worry about possible future events. The time worrying is a total waste if the feared event does not occur and if does come about, worrying had no effect in preventing the issue. It is much the same as complaining about something that no force of will can change. The weather, the actions of others, are prime examples. As to panicking in a seemingly hopeless situation, if the plane was about to crash, I did not want to waste whatever few minutes I had, paralyzed by horror. My kids looked at me with fear and tears in their eyes and my job was to calm them and ease their suffering even if only for a few moments. I also wanted to be ready to take positive action if surviving the crash or landing in water. They soon smiled along with me enjoying the antics of the uber-religious who profess a longing for heaven but are terrified of dying.

All I hoped for was capable pilots. They were. After the strike and free-falling hundreds of feet, the captain came on the speaker and said everything was under control. I told my kids, "See, all that panic and wailing did no good." To remind them that It was the pilots' skilled and steady hands, not the scores clasped in prayer that saved the plane.

Age 76 VA Hospital Philadelphia. I had a defibrillator implanted after flat lining twice in 2017. (Chapter 1) I was instructed that if I ever felt any discomfort in my chest to go right to the emergency room. It happened, and I went in as a precaution.

I have normally low blood pressure, and that information is in my medical records. I was not aware that those with low blood pressure should not be given nitroglycerine tablets. The ER doctors should have known better also but the first thing they did was put a tablet under my tongue. I crashed almost instantly. I could see only blurry images. I could not talk. I could still hear, and I was aware of what was happening around me. They called for a "crash cart" and "code blue" I could not see clearly but knew there were at least a dozen or so people in the room. I was sweating profusely, and I am very hairy. The lead doctor ordered an EKG, but the leads would not stick due to the sweat and hairiness. The technician continued to have problems attaching the leads and I heard the doctor yell, "Hurry the f**k up! Hurry the f**k up!" That's the first time I ever heard a doctor panic and curse, a female doctor at that. Some of those in the room held the leads in place with their fingers while the machine did its job.

When the report printed, the doctor uttered more scary words, "Oh my God, this is upside down." I do not know what she meant but it did not sound good. The blood pressure cuffs were on automatic and finally they noticed that my BP was critical. I'm not exactly sure what they did, but part of the solution was IV fluids. My eyes cleared up and I got my voice back. When the room cleared, one nurse said, "You sure gave us a scare." My response, "Hell, you gave me a scare, you almost killed me." She responded with "Yeah, I know." A few hours later my son took me home. None the worse for wear. I only count this one as a close call since my heart did not stop.

Military Service

"I'm not afraid of death; I just don't want to be there when it happens."
—Woody Allen

This is a part of my story that deserves introductory notes. The events would lead to the most horrific year of my life. John F Kennedy was elected President in November 1960. On January 20, 1961, he delivered his inaugural address. My mother and aunt were devoted fans and asked me to drive them to Washington DC to attend the speech. I was just 16 at the time and not greatly involved in political affairs but I liked him too. I listened to his speech with muted interest. The quote "Ask not what your country can do for you—ask what you can do for your country." became the most quoted and appreciated sentence in the entire oration. Little did I know that three other sections of the discourse would affect me, as well as over 2 million other teenagers just a few short years in the future.

"Let every nation know, whether it wishes us well or ill, that **we shall pay any price, bear any burden, meet any hardship**, support any friend, oppose any foe to assure the survival and the success of liberty.

This much we pledge--and more...

To **those people in the huts and villages of half the globe** struggling to break the bonds of mass misery, we pledge our best efforts to help them help themselves, for whatever period is required--not because the communists may be doing it, not because we seek their votes, but because it is right. If a free society cannot help the many who are poor, it cannot save the few who are rich.... Since this country was founded, each generation of Americans has been summoned to give testimony to its national loyalty. The graves of young Americans who answered the call to service surround the globe. Now, the trumpet summons us again, not as a call to bear arms, though arms we need. Not as a call to battle, though in battle we are, but a call to bear the burden of a **long twilight struggle year in and year out,** rejoicing in hope, patient in tribulation, a struggle against the common enemies of man. Tyranny, poverty, disease, and war itself…" *JFK 1961*

I highlighted the parts that the president promised the world. The phrases ***"huts and villages"***and "*we shall pay any price, bear any burden, meet any hardship, support any friend, oppose any foe"* were especially prophetic Little did I know that that the responsibility and the price of honoring the pledge would belong to millions of men and women, most of which were mere children at the time. My turn came just three years later when I received the letter that follows.

From the President of the United States

Greetings: You are hereby ordered for induction into the Armed Forces of the United States. Report to 401 N. Broad St. Philadelphia, PA on 9 Sep 1965 for forwarding to an Armed Forces Induction Station.

The order is direct, unambiguous, and cold. Recruits are "forwarded", as if they were packages, merchandise, or today's e-mails.

Wording was the least of my concerns. I was beginning an adventure that would end in two years or sooner with unpredictable consequences including severe injury or death. I had no inkling how greatly my life was about to change.

In mid-1965, I wrestled with choosing a college. I was accepted at several but was loath in deciding which to attend. My options were abruptly interrupted and rendered moot with the arrival of that letter from the Selective Service in August 1965 - Greetings; you have been inducted into the armed forces of the United States.

My choices, youth and freedom were snatched from me in an instant. The thought of fleeing to Canada or otherwise avoiding service did not enter my mind. I was called and I answered.

9 September – Induction center 401 N. Broad St. Philadelphia, PA. In the company of several hundred forlorn and generally unhappy youths, I went through the process of induction.

Early in the proceedings, inductees lined up facing a curtain that spread across the entire length of the assembly area. We were told to count off by threes. The next command was, "Every third man, step forward!" They did. Several Marine Corps DIs stepped out from behind the curtain and said, "You are now in the United States Marine Corps. Follow the Sergeant!" They were marched off, never to be seen or heard from again by the remaining two thirds of inductees. Not getting drafted into the Marine Corps was about the only positive event that day.

Shortly thereafter, we were loaded into buses and delivered to the 30th St. Train Station in North Philadelphia. Hours later, we found ourselves deep in the South and eventually at Fort Gordon, Georgia.

Coincidentally, later in my research, I discovered that the fort which would serve as my first military home and basic training site was named after General George Brown Gordon who was nicknamed "9 lives Gordon". His nickname snatched my attention. He was not-stillborn nor sickly as a child, but he surely had a knack for getting wounded. Many of the battle wounds could easily have been fatal. Especially since in that pre-antibiotic era many wounds, not considered mortal, ended up killing the patient via infection. He lived until 1904 and died at the age of 72.

In one battle, he was shot in the left leg twice. An hour later, a third musket ball ripped through his left arm, injuring tendons and muscles. A fourth round hit him in the shoulder. The wounds did not stop there. Although barely able to walk from blood loss, he tried to re-join the battle, but a fifth shot entered his cheek and shattered his jaw. He fell face down into his hat. It is said that he would have drowned in his own blood had not an earlier bullet put a hole in the hat, allowing the blood to ooze out.

Months later a hollow-based bullet (Minié ball) flew through his coat and grazed his back. In a later battle he suffered another head wound. It is not clear how he received the very bloody head wound but one report states it was from a saber cut. About two weeks before General Robert E. Lee surrendered, General Gordon received his last wound of the war. This time it was only a flesh wound to a leg.

He suffered additional infections and illnesses during the war but, despite the extreme prevalence of infections, survived them all and lived until 1904.

I side stepped my narrative and included a brief note on a Confederate General's war exploits because I found it interesting that I ended up in base named after another man who defied death more than once. He does not fit the category of the Lazarus Effect since he was never declared dead. (although some doctors said that he should have died), However, he gets at least honorable mention because of his uncanny talent to overcome injuries that should have killed him. If not the injuries themselves but the infections that surely followed, John B. Gordon - Wikipedia

The trip on the train itself was uneventful, remarkable only in the culture shock of seeing water fountains and bathrooms labeled "White Only" or "Colored Only" as the train crossed the Mason-Dixon Line. I was as shocked as the many Black (that was not the accepted term then) and Hispanic future soldiers on board. On the train, I met Jose Montalvo, a 17-year-old kid from Peru who enlisted to become an American citizen. He spoke little English, and I helped him with his language problem during the trip and later in basic training. As Latinos, we did not know which bathroom or water fountain to use. Since Jose was a little "Browner" than I, we figured it would be more prudent and safer to utilize the "Colored" facilities.

Jose and I ended up in the same basic training company. I translated as much as possible and helped him learn enough English to follow basic commands. I believe his lack of language proficiency caused him to score low in aptitude tests, which resulted in his assignment as an infantry soldier and eventual death in Vietnam. I do not mean to demean infantry soldiers. The armed services are a synergistic team with diverse job classifications, each part is as important as another. A battery of tests is used to determine which MOS (Military Occupational Specialty) the Army believes one is best qualified for. Personal requests are sometimes taken into consideration. I always wondered why anyone would request infantry training, but that was an available choice, and many opted for combat training.

I will not bore anyone with the details of basic training except for two incidents of note. I was amazed at how the young recruits were indoctrinated into developing a "killing" mentality. Every day at some point while sitting on bleachers listening to an officer speechify, we were instructed to jump up on command and yell, "KILL!" Not once, during the entire training process did I ever jump up and yell the word. Even at my young age, I realized that I could not be part of a brainwashing program.

The second event of note occurred during obstacle course training. One morning, I severely twisted my ankle and was sent to the infirmary. After X-rays, my ankle was wrapped. I was on crutches for a day or so, but since I did not want to be recycled, forced myself to continue basic even though I was in severe pain. The X-ray results will come into play later in this narration. For now, let's just say that I completed basic as scheduled.

After eight weeks of basic training and a battery of aptitude tests to determine the most suitable Military Occupational Specialty we shipped off to our Advanced Individual Training (AIT). Speaking of AIT and MOS testing, sometime during this period, some of us were notified that we qualified for Helicopter Flight Training and a chance for promotion to Warrant Officer Training. I had always dreamed of becoming a pilot after reading "Pilot Jack Knight" as a pre-teen. I jumped at the chance. Unfortunately, I failed the eye test. Military pilots need exceptional vision. In a sense, I was fortunate since I later discovered that Vietnam helicopter pilots' life expectancy was measured in minutes. I've often wondered if my ever-present life protecting aura would have served as well during an air to ground battle or landing in a hot zone to evacuate wounded GIs.

I found myself in Fort Holabird, Baltimore, MD, Army Intelligence School. The running joke was that Army Intelligence was an oxymoron, but at least, it was better than learning to be a cook, a clerk, or an infantry grunt. No disrespect intended; all are vital positions that make the Army and other armed services synergistically efficient organizations.

I trained as an Intelligence Analyst (MOS 96B20). That number became an important issue later in my military career.

Note, my previously mentioned friend, Jose Montalvo did go to Infantry training and then volunteered for additional Airborne training. Because of the additional training he arrived in 'Nam a month after I did. Sadly, he died in action in the war. I later discovered that he was a good friend of my best friend's sister, but I had never met him before my draft day.

Again, AIT details are just as boring as Basic training except for the aforementioned X-rays of my ankle. One day I had an awful toothache and went on sick call. All medical records are apparently kept in the same file. As I sat in the dentist's chair, he reached for my file and the ankle X-ray fell out of the folder. Out of curiosity, the dentist put it in the X-ray reader. He then asked, "How's your broken ankle doing?" "What broken ankle?" I asked.

It turned out that my ankle was slightly fractured in basic but never treated. I was taken to Walter Reed Military Hospital where I got a cast from my toes to my thigh. From no treatment to excessive, my thought at the time. I only wore the cast for a week or two. After further review, a military orthopedist decided it was just a hairline crack and had healed well enough to discard the cast. It was the only cast I've ever needed since I have never really broken a bone despite the three totaled vehicles and getting struck by one.

After AIT, I was assigned to the 519th Military Intelligence Battalion, Company B (Analysts) Other companies were military intelligence subdivisions such as Image Interpreters, Interrogators, Cartologists, and the highly secretive company A, which was comprised of Agents or "Spooks" as we called them.

The Battalion was based in Ft Bragg, NC where we waited for deployment to Vietnam. My company (B) was scheduled to ship out in June 1966 and most of us were looking forward to the usual 30-day leave prior to heading for the war zone.

The congruence of events may become complicated in the telling since, as events played out, I had no knowledge of what previous occurrences contributed to the general FUBAR (Fu***d Up Beyond All Repair) that ensued.

It turned out that sometime after arriving at Ft. Bragg and assigned to my company, Company A found itself short one man and not up to Order of Battle Strength. That company was scheduled to head out to Nam in Early May as all personnel were back from their 30-day leave.

One night at about 2 or 3 am, a squad of MPs entered my barracks, yelling my name and waking up the entire company. They were looking for me. I had no idea what was going on but still identified myself. Two or three of the brutes grabbed me and I believe my feet never hit the ground until I was dropped at the feet of Lt. Col. Johnson at Company A HQ. I was dressed only in my military issue civvies, shorts, and T-shirt. The colonel immediately began to fire questions at me, the main one being "Where the F*ck, have you been, we've been looking for you for a month?" I have a unique talent for not panicking but was still in some level of shock and incredulity. I said, "Sir, I've been across the street in company B barracks since AIT. I'm just waiting for my 30-day leave."

"You're not going anywhere; we leave for Nam in six days." He said.

"That can't be, I need to see my family before I ship out." I answered.

The colonel in some semblance of pity seemed to have understood that the mistake was not mine and that I had not been purposely AWOL. He did, however, in an effort to display no weakness, pushed me against the wall and sternly advised me that he would let me go home for three days but if I was not back in the allotted time, he would have every MP in Philadelphia looking for me.

I had no choice, so I agreed. They quickly arranged for a seat on Piedmont Airlines (A primitive company whose planes felt like death traps, but again, my options were limited.) My whirlwind leave was greatly appreciated. On day 3, I almost missed the return flight due to circumstances beyond my control. A truckload of pigs overturned on the expressway and the escaped swine stopped traffic for miles. A friend who coincidentally was also on leave prior to Vietnam drove me to the airport and expertly found alternate routes.

We arrived just barely in time. The door to my assigned plane was getting ready to close. There was no TSA at the time so there was no laborious security check before boarding. I took off running to my gate without the opportunity to give my parents a proper goodbye, no hugs or handshakes. The rickety plane took off noisily and I had to look out the window to verify that the wings were not flapping. Coincidently, my youngest grandson starts work for Piedmont Airlines as an airplane mechanic in about a month.

Landing at Fayetteville, North Carolina a jeep awaited me on the tarmac and from there began a flurry of activity to prepare for the next adventure. I was still not aware of the background intrigue that caused the removal from my company and transfer to the Spooks' company. I should have gotten a hint since I was ordered to buy civilian clothes, had to qualify with a .38 detective special, directed to not salute officers, disregard my rank and answer only to "Mister." At no time did anyone ever explain what had transpired, or why. I was expected to follow along as if I were part of, or cognizant of the sinister plan.

I had been with my original company for months, with some as far back as basic training and through AIT. Many were considered friends with some that became life-long. I knew no one in Company A and I was a bit of an outcast. The Agents were all "RA" (Regular Army or 4-year volunteers) their service numbers were prefixed with RA while inductees carried A US designation before their serial numbers. Also, they all were college graduates and most notably, all Caucasian. I was the only Hispanic in the entire unit, including the HQ department which handles the mundane paperwork. Note that this was before the Civil Rights Act was enforceable. I do not believe I spoke more than three words to any of the agents, except officers, if they addressed me first, during my entire association with that company.

Vietnam
1965 to 1967

"A single death is a tragedy; a million deaths is a statistic."—Joseph Stalin

On arrival to the Southeast Asia paradise, the weather reminded me of my original island home. I was glad that summer was eternal, and I would not have to deal with cold or marching through foot deep snowfalls as my uncles did in Korea and Europe.

Aside from the weather, there was not much else to celebrate. Fortunately, we did not land as the troops did on D-Day under a hail of machine gun fire and mortar rounds but had to run from the C-130 transport planes to board waiting trucks. We could see our jets and helicopters blasting away in a battle just a few miles distant. The trucks we boarded took us to the Battalion's home base 25 miles from Saigon in the middle of nowhere.

519th MI Battalion Headquarters was a nice sized compound protected by a river and barbed wire all along our side of the river bank and high walls on the other three sides. Military muscle was provided by an infantry detachment, which conducted periodic patrols, covered the machine gun towers, and provided security for the Intelligence unit. However, we were all armed and expected to participate in any emergency. I was M-60 qualified just in case. During an assault, my assignment was a machine gun tower if needed to replace any injured machine gunner during an assault.

I travelled from the US in the company of uncommunicative strangers and remained more or less solitary during the trip. On arrival at the in-country compound, I saw some uniformed GIs and noticed a Spanish nametag. "Damn, I'm home," I thought. I introduced myself and found out that they were part of the infantry detachment. There were ten of them; all Boricuas, from my home island and their squad leader was Sgt. E-5 Medina. Later that day, all gathered to welcome me to the compound and help me acclimate to conditions. The group, now numbering eleven, met at the NCO club in the compound. Medina wore a magnificent handlebar mustache, which was the thing to do in those days. Most drank heavily, since there was not much to do in Nam except drink and visit houses of ill-repute when not patrolling, standing guard, or, in my case, nose deep in documents and reports (I still believed I was an analyst).

I do not drink but that was not held against me. We talked through the evening until the NCO club closed. We each went to our respective tents or Quonset huts.

I had just laid my head on my pillow, under which I kept my issued revolver. I instantly grabbed it at hearing the first gunshot.

All manner of dark thoughts entered my head – I'm going to die on my first night, all I have is a five shot tiny revolver while everyone else carries an M-14 (the M-16 was not available yet) and the enemy were armed with AK-47s. As mentioned earlier, I tend not to panic during adverse situations but am subject to fearsome thoughts. I ran to the door and opened it carefully. No one else had moved yet, I assumed they were accustomed to occasional gunfire. I stepped outside in my underwear.

I saw a soldier on the ground. To my right I saw Sgt Medina running to the prone body and empty his M-14 rapid fire into the soldier on the ground. To my left, the compound gate guard fired once hitting Medina in the leg. All this took mere milliseconds and in that brief period, it was difficult to assess the entire situation, especially as inexperienced as I was. My only thought was, "we're killing each other."

I have replayed that scene in my head countless times, and it is still incomprehensible. As the hours passed, the facts became clear. My newfound friend and brief mentor, Medina, was drunk and wanted more. The guard at the gate did not allow him to leave the compound to visit the local bar/whorehouse down the road from the base. Since

Sgt Medina outranked the guard, the guard called the Sergeant of the Guard, SFC Birdsong who told Medina, "Go back to your tent, drink again tomorrow." That request did not please him. Medina went to his tent, got his M-14, fired the first shot from a distance and that was the shot that stirred me from my bunk.

It was a difficult day that followed, especially since I was one of the two witnesses to the fragging except for the first shot, which I heard but did not see. For those not familiar with the term "fragging," it describes the act of shooting a fellow soldier, usually a higher ranking one on purpose to settle a real or imagined dispute/insult/disrespect. Fragging usually occurs during a firefight when it is difficult to determine who shot whom.

The band of Latino brothers was now short one and we spent many sad days recuperating from the shock. SFC Birdsong's death was listed as the result of "friendly fire." The main problem was that the "friendly" fire was by our friend and real friendly fire is usually accidental. The number of the group would diminish as tragedy moved inexorably to remind us of where we were and keep us from becoming complacent. This event should not have been declared "Friendly Fire" since that term is used when planes drop bombs or rockets near their own troops. Also, when field commanders call for artillery fire on their own position when in danger of being overrun. This was a liquor induced murder. Later, I discovered that the military brass reported that the cause was an escaped prisoner of war, but no prisoners of any kind were held in our camp.

Sgt. Medina was eventually found guilty on all counts and sentenced to life in prison.

A few days after the shooting, my civilian status and membership in the elite Company A came to an abrupt end. The unit was ordered to meet in the NCO club to receive duty assignments. When the Lt. colonel in charge called my name, I met him at a table, where he explained that I would be heading to a northern province with a partner and would get details there. I glanced at my open file and gasped when I saw that my MOS had been changed to 97B20 when it should have been 96B20. I told him my MOS was altered. The colonel said, "You're not an agent? I told him, "No. I am an analyst." The officer appeared to get very angry but calmed down to ask me how I got into Company A. I gave him a rundown of my experience since my assignment to the Battalion. Fortunately, he agreed that I was not to blame nor responsible for the mysterious transfer or adjustment of records. He called it a real Army "clusterf*ck."

The most logical explanation was that the agents' company was short one man to be at "Order of Battle" strength. (Note: Order of Battle strength refers to personnel and equipment required before entering a war zone.) It was not determined why my name had been selected. I would like to believe it was due to superlative test scores or some other talent I was not aware of, but it could have been as simple as picking a name out of a hat.

No matter the reason, I was free from them. I was told to wait until my original unit of analysts arrived in Vietnam. An unexpected problem arose when I found out that, while I had been physically transferred, some of my records or files had not. In other words, I would receive no pay until the records, or my old company caught up to me in a month or so. I also had no uniforms.

I continued to pretend, or at least not mention, that I was no longer in civilian status or a spook. Since just about everyone in the compound carried "secret" clearance, very few questions were asked or answered. A secret clearance also carries the "need to know" proviso. I also hated to salute and while everybody knew (or thought) that I was an agent; no one questioned my disregard for military protocol. There was one, Sergeant Brown, who suspected and asked why I was still there when Company A had left days ago. I told him to speak to the Battalion commander and that I was not obligated to answer to anyone. He never went up the chain of command but watched me like a hawk. I was still receiving mail as "mister" since I never received orders to the contrary. I wrote home and asked my parents to send some cash since I was not being paid. One of the few benefits of serving in a war zone is that mail is free, no postage required.

Every day most of the battalion would leave the compound in a convoy and travel to the Intelligence center in Ton Son Nhut Air Base in Saigon, accompanied by an attachment of the infantry unit assigned to defend our compound and escort us during the trip.

One day I hitched a ride on a transport vehicle and went to Intel HQ in Ton Son Nhut Airport where I met with the Colonel in charge and actually asked for a job after explaining my ordeal and boredom. He was a very nice man, but I kept an eye on the Thompson Sub Machine gun on his desk. He noticed my interest and explained that the air base was subject to periodic assaults, mostly brief mortar attacks, and the occasional sapper. The colonel told me he could do nothing for me until my records showed up, but I was welcome to visit the base whenever I wanted. I did have my ID, indicating "Secret" clearance.

Although the trip to the base in jeeps and ¾ ton trucks was perilous, I made frequent trips to ease the boredom, plus the base had a huge pool, which I used on occasion. One day, sitting on the edge of the pool, a soldier came over and sat right beside me. I did not recognize him at first (he had grown much more than I had since we last saw each other.) He mentioned my name and said, "It's me Julio, don't you recognize me?" We had been friends almost since birth until his family moved to another city when we were teenagers. It all came back in a flash. He was stationed at the base doing helicopter maintenance. His main job was maintaining a bird colonel's helicopter and as such could use it pretty much at will. He travelled frequently to Vung Tau, an in-country R&R (Rest and Relaxation) with a great beach, relatively safe and the cleanest places for female companionship. He invited me to join him on his frequent trips, which turned into regular adventures.

The Vung Tau flight was relatively short but thrilling. Helicopter pilots are among the most fearless men I met in the service. Our regular pilot assumed that we were just as fearless and had no problem evaluating our resolve flying at tree top level and inviting enemy fire. The chopper had a door mounted M-60, which I was qualified to use, but I never got the opportunity to fire a shot in anger or for fun. It was especially fearsome after The Stars and Stripes (Military Newspaper) published an article on helicopter warfare. The idiotic report included diagrams and detailed instructions on the most efficient way the VC could shoot down helicopters. I talked to him about the article. He did not care. It was his chopper, and he would fly it any way he wanted.

Julio and I lost contact after we were discharged but reconnected a couple of years later through a mutual acquaintance. He is not doing well due to Agent Orange complications that I've been able to overcome. Additional sad news is that his younger brother lost both legs in Vietnam and his older brother died also due to the murderous Agent Orange.

My original unit arrived as expected. I spent days telling my story to my old friends. My records arrived as well as my personal duffel bag full of uniforms. I was back in the uniformed element of the US Army, not the clandestine unit that kept me hostage for weeks. It took a few days to sort out the paperwork, but no one was ever able to explain the series of events that occurred. They either could not or would not.

I was back in business with my original company, and everything proceeded as if nothing unusual had happened. Routine soon set in. Every day we would leave the compound in convoy fashion, travelling 25 miles or so to Tan Son Nhut Air base where the actual intelligence work was done. On more than a few occasions, our convoy encountered enemy fire driving through thick woods on either side of the road or while driving through a busy marketplace. One day driving the Lieutenant's jeep and following a ¾-ton truck, I saw a guerrilla step out and throw a grenade into the truck in front of my jeep. The quick-thinking soldiers sitting in the back jumped out and suffered only minor shrapnel wounds. The assailant blended into the crowd and escaped while we continued on our way minus one vehicle.

I was placed in charge of the Military Personalities Unit whose task was to identify enemy commanders, study the unit's Order of Battle strength, tactics, equipment, location, and movements. Image interpreters studied aerial photographs to verify location. Interrogators provided results of POW interrogations and interview results from field operatives. Reports also came in from my former temporary Company A, and I wondered if I could have faked it and done the job without endangering my assigned partner or myself.

Vietnam was far more dangerous for the infantry or the special units that were in the field conducting search and destroy missions and subject to attack on a daily basis. Helicopter pilots carried a short life expectancy. Jet and recon pilots were also in constant danger. In a guerrilla war, almost every single US Serviceman was a target for the enemy. From suicide bombers, solo grenade throwers or snipers to wholesale assaults anywhere in the country, every soldier had to be on constant alert.

Across the river from our encampment, a sniper routinely fired several shots into the compound on a regular basis. In the year I was there, he never hit anyone, but we could never find him either. He was not a great shot but was an expert at hiding. The closest he got was a bullet that came through the roof of our Quonset hut. One weekend afternoon, I was lying on my bunk reading. One of my friends was doing the same in the adjoining bunk. I heard a ping and looked over to my buddy who had turned ashen and unable to speak. He had a sheet covering his legs and I saw smoke coming from between his legs. The bullet hit just below his private parts, but the hole was in the thin mattress and not his person. It took him a while to recover from the shock, but we had a good laugh afterwards.

Speaking of private parts, as noted earlier, there was not much to do after regular duties except drink or seek some sexual satisfaction. The average age of Vietnam soldiers was 19 and most had little control of hormonal agitations. Although dangerous, trips to nearby Saigon were common. Tu Do Street was famous for the number of pleasure houses as has been the rule ever since soldiers are assigned for duty in foreign countries. One in particular was considered very high quality but due to its popularity, there was a time limit. Each room had an alarm clock that started the minute the customer entered the room. It was a classic case of "slam, bang, thank you ma'am." I only went there once. I Do not like being rushed. On arrival in 'Nam I heard that one way to avoid STDs was to pee immediately after sex. I do not know if that is true, but the advice made sense since it is logical to assume that invading microbes can be washed away while in the urethra before they find a nice safe place to settle in, replicate and begin the invasion process in the host body.

The alarm-limited escapade did not even allow for a bathroom break before or after. I needed to safeguard myself and fortunately, on leaving the establishment I was met by a veritable monsoon as soon as I stepped into the street. I was soaked almost instantly so I just relieved myself as I walked, and the raging rain washed away any possible microscopic invaders.

Many soldiers were not so fortunate due to failure to use protection or take post coital defensive measures. One young man, only 17 at the time, got an infection that caused his genitals to swell to gigantic proportions. (Elephantiasis: the enlargement of body parts due to tissue swelling often caused by parasitic worm infections – Wikipedia). Just the touch of a sheet would cause intense pain, so he just lay there, spread-eagled and fully exposed. I think the abuse he got from insensitive GIs was worse than the disease. He eventually recovered but with a war story too embarrassing to share.

During duty hours, I was busy working with my fellow analysts and associates. In the evenings at Battalion headquarters, I maintained contact with my fellow islanders. Most of the conversations revolved around what we would do when we got "back to the world." Some planned their out of country R&R and argued as to which destination was best. The choices were Tokyo, Thailand, Australia, and others. I had no need for out-of-country R&R because I could visit Vung Tau with my buddy Julio whenever we had a free day or two.

An R&R trip turned into a tragic experience for two of my Boricua brothers. One of my friends asked me to get a jeep and drive him to Tan Son Nhut airport. I was on an assignment and could not go. He asked two of the other Puerto Rican soldiers to take him. They did, but on the way back from dropping him off, they chose to go joy riding off road. We found them several days later in conditions that are too horrible to describe. I wondered at times, why my native island compatriots seemed to have targets painted on their backs. Of the original eleven, only two of us made it through the year without drastic or fatal circumstances.

It is especially true of combat soldiers who engage in battle on a regular basis that they cannot afford complacency or carelessness at any time. Those of us who saw action sporadically were sometimes lulled into a somnolent state where attention is dulled, and the self-preservation instinct gets lost in the subconscious. It is amazing how a few well-placed enemy mortar rounds can snap one back into the reality and horror of war.

On December 4th, 1966, Vietcong sappers attacked Ton Son Nhut Airbase. The first wave was with mortar shells and later an armed assault including sappers. As the mortar rounds were "walked in," it felt as if a giant was stomping his way to our position. "Walking in" mortars is when an observer high in a tree or high ground watches where a mortar hits, then advises the crew to raise their aim a click or two, until the preferred target is reached. As each mortar hit closer to the Intelligence building, a few soldiers lost any semblance of duty and courage. Some cried; others called for their moms, and a few even became paralyzed into inaction. Fear, especially that of impending death, has a way of eliminating pride, inhibitions and even control of bodily functions. It was more acceptable if a newly arrived soldier lost his cool but not for an experienced one. Just like old war movies, some soldiers had to be slapped around to "get in the game." It didn't always work. One or two still ended up cowering in a corner.

Everyone had a pre-assigned position or function in the event of an assault. The colonel with his always-handy Thompson submachine gun covered us while some climbed into machine gun towers. My issued weapons at the time were a .38 Caliber snub-nose revolver from my "agent" days and an M-14. A freshly arrived 17-year-old took a position with me at a window to watch for any who made it past our initial defenses. The kid was almost ready to cry but did fine. Some others succumbed to their fears and did not do so well.

The incoming forces were still at a good distance. The airbase had a perimeter of over 13 miles, and we had the decided advantage of air power readily available. Assault helicopters and jets scrambled to the outer edges. I managed to fire off a few bursts at those who managed to get through but cannot say with certainty if I hit anyone since there were others firing away in the same direction. The assault began in late afternoon and was active all night. When dark, helicopters dropped flares and the place lit up like a sunrise in the Caribbean. My young companion said exuberantly, "Wow, now we can see them!" I responded with, "You ass, now they can see us too!" One of the mortars managed a direct hit on our building and a window near mine shattered. The young soldier with me jumped at the impact and fell on shattered window glass. He got a minor cut in one hand but bled enough to earn a Purple Heart. It was almost a direct hit on my position, but I won't add it as one of my close calls. The walls of our building were pretty solid.

Viet Cong attack on Tan Son Nhut Air Base (1966)
<u>Viet Cong attack on Tan Son Nhut Air Base (1966) |</u>
<u>Military Wiki | Fandom</u>

This was the first and last assault on the base during my tour of duty. There was another one the following year in the 1968 Tet offensive.

In defiance of the danger to the base in the December 1966 attack, US MACV (Military Assistance Command Vietnam) Commanders did not improve base security. They were under the impression that any enemy attack could be easily discovered and repelled before they entered the interior of the base. They were wrong. A year and a month later, on 31 January 1968, The Viet Cong attacked with a larger force. The battle was more severe than the one I was in. In that assault, twenty-two Americans were killed along with twenty-nine Vietnamese soldiers lost. The attacking VC forces lost 669 men. Gladly, I was not there at the time.

After this battle, MACV learned their lesson and initiated stronger defensive measures, not only in Ton Son Nhut, but in all in-country airbases. Heavy equipment included more mortar emplacements, and machine guns mounted on armored vehicles instead of jeeps. M50 Machine guns and M-67 recoilless rifles were also added to the defensive arsenal. It was a typical case of too little too late.

The Air Force Base was finally taken during the fall of Saigon which occurred March 4 to April 30, 1975, it was the last major event of the war.

My tour continued with the occasional skirmish at Battalion HQ as well as the sniper who never hit anyone or the occasional very brief encounters on the route to and from the Intelligence center. I lost a few more friends along the way but notably those from PR who appeared to be ill fated as a group. Medina may still be in jail, two ambushed while joy riding. One, with, just two in country days remaining, over celebrated with booze and drugs and was taken out in a strait jacket. Five others were killed or injured in various incidents. Only Kiko and I made it out with no physical injuries. Psychologically, I'm still not sure.

All wars are brutal with little or no compassion for or from either side. The Vietnam conflict was unusual in that soldiers sent to battle in the so-called "defense of their country" were, for a time, unappreciated, un-thanked and even subject to abuse on returning home. My Peruvian friend who died in the hope of easing his path toward citizenship might have regretted his choice had he encountered the reception some returnees experienced. My alma mater, Edison HS, reportedly suffered more alumni casualties than any other HS in the country. Many were in my graduating class.

I suppose that my first night was not unusual, nor the worst possible scenario. Many suffered greater indignities or injuries. Whether it was their first or last day does not matter. Irreparable injuries to body and mind are often carried for a lifetime, sometimes silently. Far too many made the ultimate sacrifice. Lives unfulfilled and unnoticed, except for their names etched on a black granite wall.

Business and Law Enforcement

"The life you have left is a gift. Cherish it. Enjoy it now, to the fullest. Do what matters, now."—Leo Babauta

In the last few days in Vietnam, I was interrogated de-briefed and advised by two officers. One set of advisories was to remind me that I had a "Secret" clearance, and I was not to discuss any of my duties or anything related to Intelligence information. The other was to make me an offer, they believed I could not refuse. The offer was 30-day leave. Immediate promotion to E-5 (sergeant) and $7,000 cash I wanted to laugh but just smiled and said Thank you, but NO! I did not even consider that I could have purchased three brand new Ford Mustangs or a top-of-the-line Corvette and have change left over. Interesting, that less than two years later, I did buy a brand-new Corvette Sting Ray.

I was even more glad at rejecting the offer since on my return from Vietnam in 1967, I found that my father had lost his job. He was a great mechanic but due to his age, he could not get a good job. I had saved most of my pay from the service and also got a nice "mustering out" bonus.

With what I called my Vietnam blood money, I decided to open a service station. My father would take care of mechanical repairs while I pumped the gas and managed the business. It worked out far better than I expected. Within three years, I owned three service stations with as many as 28 employees.

Although I was doing well with my own business, I had always dreamed of becoming a police officer. The opportunity came up in 1968. The city announced an exam to find qualified people who wanted to become police officers. I scored in the top five out of about twenty-seven thousand applicants.

In the fifties, sixties and even the seventies, the racial climate did not favor African Americans or Hispanics. There was talk of something called "Affirmative Action" defined as "…a policy aimed at increasing workplace and educational opportunities for people who are underrepresented in various areas of our society. (and) seeks to reverse historical trends of discrimination against individuals with certain identities." The program was introduced due to the 1964 Civil Rights Act.

It was believed that white applicants with higher scores could be skipped over to get to a lower scoring Black or Hispanic candidate. I'm not sure if that was the actual practice, but in my case, no one would need to be skipped to get to me since many recruits were needed and I was near the top of the list.

Unfortunately, racism was still rampant in many lines of work, including the police department.

All who scored over a certain number would then be required to pass a physical, background investigation, polygraph, and drug test. The physical and eye exams were conducted by medical personnel. All the other tests were in the hands of police officers including height and weight. In those days, the minimum height was five feet seven inches.

When the officers checking height and weight saw me, they took me out of the line and moved me to an adjacent room. I was in socks and underwear, but they had me remove my socks and inspected the soles of my feet to make sure I had not packed anything under my heels. They then directed me to a wall resembling a line-up wall with numbered lines in feet and inches. There were three cops in the room with me. They backed me up to the wall and one officer went to his hands and knees to make sure I did not raise my heels. Another cop pushed my head down so I could not stretch my neck. The third one stared at the wall chart. As soon as the top of my head went below the 5'7" mark he yelled, "he's sub normal, get him the fu*ck out of here." I got dressed and went home. Coming out of the building, a white cop walked by me who was clearly shorter than I was. I did not make an issue of it. I was no Rosa Parks. What upset me the most was that four other applicants had outscored me in the written test.

I still had my business and joining the force would have meant a huge pay cut. My cousin went through the same experience, but he fought back in court and won. He advanced to the rank of Lieutenant and retired as a highly decorated officer.

This part of my life story will continue ten years later.

Returning to my business, I enjoyed some fruitful years. I did stumble a few times making mistakes that proved costly in the long run. I was 22 years old and believed that I had full control of my finances and business. My father kept telling me to invest, buy some properties or just save. I told him, "Pop, if I make it today, I can make it tomorrow." I was wrong. I did not realize at the time that most, if not all businesses can be influenced by events in other parts of the world.

On November 4, 1979, the American Embassy in Iran was overrun and seized by Iranian students. That act started a domino effect that created an oil and gasoline crisis in the US. Gasoline was rationed and to lessen panic buying and long lines at gas stations, the odd and even tag system was employed. Cars with tags ending in an even number could buy gas on Monday, Wednesday, and Friday. Odd number ending tags could gas up on Tuesday, Thursday, and Saturday. Sunday was free for all. Even with this program, cars waiting their turn for gas lined up for blocks, sometimes waiting for hours.

The shortages not only affected the general population, but businesses as well, especially those directly affected by oil and gas shortages. Much of my business income was provided by gasoline sales. If no gasoline could be delivered, I could not sell it.

Because I had failed to heed my father's warnings, I had not saved much money. The well was running dry. I had to lay off some people and sold my Corvette in hopes that the Iran crisis would end soon, and I could save my business. I also attempted to sell my interest in the service stations, but it was not a safe investment at the time. I considered bankruptcy too, but something happened in late 1978 that offered a second chance.

The city announced a new examination for the Police Department. This exam was not for patrol officers but for police dispatchers. I jumped at it anyway. By then the racial climate had eased somewhat and due to lawsuits, newer equal employment opportunities, the height requirements were eliminated, allowing more women and shorter men to apply. I took the test again. This time I placed #21 on the eligibility list. Sixteen spots lower than my score ten years earlier. I wondered if I had lost some mental acuity since 1968. I later found out that applicants with equal scores were placed on the list using the stamped dates of submissions on the applications as a tiebreaker.

I spent five years with the police department, but I was a single parent, and the swing shifts were an unbearable burden. I then heard that the Sheriff's Office was hiring. The jobs were different but not greatly. I switched sides and never regretted the change. Police handle criminal law while Deputies deal with criminal and civil law.

On the criminal side, police handle suspected criminals until they are arraigned or charged. The Sheriff then takes over the responsibility of transporting prisoners to and from court. If out on bail and do not appear in court or escapes, a fugitive warrant is issued, and it is the Sheriff's job to find him/her and return the wanted person back to jail. The best part for my son and me was that the job was all day work with weekends and holidays off. Except for special details, Sheriffs in Philadelphia do not patrol the streets nor issue traffic citations, so it is relatively safer.

As the Iran crisis simmered down, I eased out my business and concentrated on the new job. I tried to remain in business but the double duty would have hurt one or the other. Also, my pay was enough for my needs and the work was much more enjoyable. It was the dream job that I had always wanted. The only disappointment was that I should have been hired ten years earlier.

As my son grew older, I took on different facets of the job. My favorite was as a member of the Fugitive Warrant Unit. If a prisoner escapes or if he skips a court date while on bail and is arrested in another state, the authorities of that state call and ask if we still want him. Two deputies either fly or drive to that jurisdiction to retrieve the wanted person.

My favorite trips were to my home island, Puerto Rico, where I could visit friends and relatives for at least a few hours. Other perks included occasional upgrades to first class when flying out to pick up a fugitive or flying back after delivering one. We were always armed. When traveling with a prisoner, we always boarded first. The prisoner was handcuffed but his hands were covered with a jacket or sweater so as not to frighten the passengers. We sat in the last row with the prisoner in the middle seat. No bathroom calls unless it was a very long flight. I am proud to say that my partner and I never had an escape or even an attempted one.

My years as a Deputy Sheriff were interesting, exciting, and dangerous at times but the kind of job that I enjoyed getting up in the morning for. I've already mentioned a couple of perilous events, the shotgun pointed at my face and the shooting of a young man just feet from me. As a member of the Fugitive Warrant Unit, I had to arrest fugitives that were not too willing to go back to jail. Occasional foot chases were inevitable. I trained by running 3 miles, three times a week and training for 5 kilometer running events usually held for Law Enforcement Officers. The problem was that the fugitives avoiding arrest were usually younger and faster than I was, but they had less stamina. As long as I kept them in sight, I was confident that I would eventually catch up with them when they tired. I must admit that on a few occasions a younger officer was in position to take over the chase and give me some relief. It became a little more difficult as I got older while the equipment, I carried did not get any lighter. The utility belt included a gun, mace, handcuffs, and taser. Increasing the handicap was the heavy body armor and not wearing running shoes. One brief, but fun chase was when the young man we were looking for jumped out of a second story window dressed only in bikini underwear on a cold wet day. He only ran a block before diving under a pickup truck. Unfortunately for him, he dove into a pile of dog poop. Amusing, but unfortunate for the lowest ranked officer since he had to cuff the soiled stinky felon. As an unearned courtesy, we walked him back to his home and allowed his family to wipe him down and get him some clothes before we put him in our prisoner van.

One of my favorite assignments was visiting schools to talk to kids about the danger of drugs and assuring them that law enforcement officers were not the enemy. The kids loved it more when we brought our K-9 dogs to put on a display on how they could locate hidden drugs in minutes. The officer and his dog waited outside the classroom while another officer concealed a small sample of a controlled substance. Entering the room, the dog was set loose to sniff around. Usually in one circling of the room, the dog signaled he'd found something. The kids clapped and some were allowed to pet the dog. The officers then took turns answering questions. The first question from boys was usually, "Can we see your gun?" Or "Have you shot anybody?" The answer to both was always," No."

The best two visits to schools were when the classes selected were the ones where my grandson and granddaughter were students. I only had two of them at the time. I now have 6 grand and 10 great grands with one more on the way.

Another program we had for older kids was called "scared straight." We brought students, usually boys who had a history of being disruptive in school, into our cell room area and were treated as if they were prisoners. There are no statistics to show if that program was effective or not.

Retirement

"Life should not be a journey to the grave with the intention of arriving safely in a pretty and well-preserved body, but rather to skid in broadside in a cloud of smoke, thoroughly used up, totally worn out, and loudly proclaiming "Wow! What a Ride!"
—Hunter S. Thompson

The last few years of employment became more difficult due to the progress of my Agent Orange induced ailments; I had no choice but to retire early. Most criminals are 18 to 35 years old and while I was still in decent shape, a chase or direct confrontation with a much younger felon might have proven problematic. I turned in my badge and since the US Government and Veterans Administration had already classified me as disabled, retired on disability.

To keep busy, I developed an interest in Genealogy and DNA. I began with my own ancestral history. The first step was to get my DNA tested to discover the recipe detailing the varied ethnicities that by chance, accident, or deliberate conquest combined to end up with me. I was familiar with the major portions of my genealogical makeup but wanted a more detailed list.

My ancestry is 63 percent Southern European, mostly from the Iberian Peninsula (Spain). The next largest ingredient is 17.1 percent Indigenous American, more specifically Caribbean Taino Indians. The remainder is divided among various African Tribes, Ashkenazi Jewish, Broadly European, Mesopotamian, Arab, Iranian, Egyptian, Levantine, Broadly Western Asian, and my favorite – 3% Neanderthal. Other investigations indicated elements of Scotch-Irish. British and other European based lineage.

That is one hell of a melting pot, but that is not unusual. Ethnic purity is very rare. Let's do a little math. If you count backwards starting with 2 parents, 4 grandparents, 8 great-grandparents and so on – In twenty generations, roughly four hundred years, you'll see that it took 1,047,136 people (ancestors) to end up with you. Notice also that not everyone has a separate, distinct list of 1 million plus ancestors. During the past twenty generations, there must have been some sharing of MtDNA (maternal) and/or YDNA (paternal) with those of other ethnicities.

Most people forget or choose to ignore that just a few hundred years ago countries engaged in wars of conquest (even now). France would invade England, Spain invaded Italy (Sicily belonged to Spain for about 300 years) and likewise, the Moors occupied Spain. European, Asian and Middle East nations took turns invading each other. And what do invading armies do, they rape, pillage and burn while spreading their seed. It has been reported that one in 200 people in the world carry Genghis Khan DNA. Not sure if that is true but according to my own Genome report, I'm one them.

I mentioned earlier that my brother's nickname was (and is) Caveman. As soon as I downloaded my DNA breakdown, I called and told him, "You really are a Caveman!"

As I write this, there are State Governors and other mis-informed and mis-guided politicians who want to ban books and alter or edit history books in the fear that the current generation may be embarrassed of, or shamed by the actions of long dead ancestors.

Speaking for myself, I am who I am because over 500 years ago Caucasian Explorers from Spain stumbled onto the island of Boriquen. (Puerto Rico) and claimed the "discovery" for Spain. I've always wondered how an island, or any other land can be discovered when it was already occupied by hundreds of thousands, if not millions for over ten thousand years.

They took possession of the island and set out to brutalize the Indigenous population. They worked to death or outright killed many of the males but kept the women as concubines. I am among the many descendants of that blending, usually by force. I am (mostly) the result of Conquistadores and those they conquered. I am not ashamed of, nor dislike either side. I do not approve of what the Spaniards (and other conquerors) did, nor do I approve of the Taino Indians' subservience who allowed themselves to be abused, mainly due to religious beliefs and naiveté. They treated the "visitors" like gods. By sheer force of numbers, the natives could easily have defeated the newcomers and sunk their ships. Another expedition may have come later with perhaps different outcomes, but I would not currently exist…well, not this version of me.

I spent many hours searching the internet trying to document my lineage as far back as possible. I can verify my paternal surname as far back as 1665 to my father's hometown of Arecibo. A Spanish Captain Antonio De Los Reyes Correa, was in charge of a unit of the Puerto Rican Militia in that city when the British invaded with a company sized force while two big ships remained offshore. Reyes Correa only had 30 men in his unit armed with machetes and pitchforks but by the end of the battle 28 British troops were dead on the beach and another 8 in the surf including their captain. It appears that the invading force was armed with muskets, but they may have tried to fire while in the water and could not aim accurately due to the waves rocking their little row boats. An active ocean is fine for surfing but not for accurate aiming. Some of the militia met the invaders by wading out to fight them in the water. The remaining attackers headed back to their ships and sailed off.

Reyes Correa was wounded in the skirmish, but he was honored as a hero. He was named Captain of Infantry. It was customary to elevate those with that title to Mayor of the city. In later years he gained the position on his own merit and served several terms. He is still honored as a hero in my hometown.

I carry that surname proudly. On my genealogical research, I travelled to Southern Spain to the town where I had read that was the origin of that surname. I parked in the town plaza and set out to look for the local church which historically maintained records of every birth, baptismal, marriage and death.

A young woman passed by me and saw me looking around. She asked, "Que busca? (What are you looking for?) I answered, "La iglesia para investigar mi appellido." (The church so I can research my surname.)

"O si, que nombre busca?' (Oh yes, what name are you looking for?)

I said, "Reyes."

She laughed and said, "Yo soy Reyes." (I am Reyes)

I was dumbfounded. The first person I met in that foreign city happened to share my last name.

I did not make it to the church genealogy files that day. The young lady and I stopped at a small coffee shop and spent a couple of hours talking about history, surnames, the beauty of Spain and our respective backgrounds. We both wondered if we were distant relatives 500 years removed. That encounter made my trip worthwhile. Unfortunately, that was many years before instant communication via cell phones and e-mail and we could not maintain contact. I've continued my research and have created a many branched family tree.

Higher Education

"It's so much darker when a light goes out than it would have been if it had never shone."—*John Steinbeck*

As I grew older, I took on several projects that had always interested me. One was writing. I began to write articles for local newspapers and on-line publications. I wrote public service articles, Opinion pieces, and articles on voting, police affairs and political opinion. At one point, a Midwest online news service offered me a job. I filled out the application and prepared to start a new career as a journalist. This paper had already published a few of my articles, so I believed I'd be starting soon.

I received a call from the editor asking me what my college degree was in. I told him I did not have a degree, just a High School Diploma. He said, "To be hired you need a degree." I asked, "Why, you already publish my work?"

"No." he said, "As a guest writer we can publish what you send, but as an employee, you need a degree in English, Journalism or a related field."

"OK, no problem," And I ended the call.

Before getting drafted I planned to enroll in college, but waited too long and got the dreaded notice. After discharge, I believed I was too old to go back to school. I had considered the idea of getting a degree for a years, but life went on and I felt I had no need.

I then found out that the VA had started a program for Vets on disability to get a college degree as a sort of re-hab program or maybe even get employed. The opportunity was too good to pass up. I jumped in. Found an online course on Communication and Journalism. The VA paid all costs, provided a new laptop, printer, and a monthly check. I returned to school well into my sixties.

That is the reason why the chapter on higher education follows the one on retirement.

I enjoyed it at first, but part of the education regimen called for "Team Learning" which means exactly that. Students must form groups of five or more and work on assigned projects. Most of the other students were significantly younger than I. After a few sessions I ended up as the leader of each team learning group mainly because of my age and frankly, because I had a lifetime of experience and reading up on a variety of fields.

I did not believe I could go on for four years dealing with students that were a quarter my age. I was even older than most of the professors. I then made a fascinating discovery – CLEP which stands for College Level Examination Program. It is a fabulous program that allows one to get college credits by testing out of classes. If able to pass what is equivalent to a Final Exam, the test results in credits for that subject without wasting a minute in class. Each successful exam produces at least six credits, equaling a five- or six-week class. The logic is simple – why waste time in a class, studying a subject you already have adequate proficiency in?

Let me back up a little. My mother gave my brother and me the most valuable gift a child could get. She taught us how to read and write while still toddlers. I started first grade just before I turned four. The school permitted it because I knew how to read, and they had allowed my brother in when he was four and also able to read. That early start gave us both a voracious appetite for reading, The lessons were in Spanish of course, so we would have to learn to speak, read, and write a new language a few years later. The alphabet is identical to English, so it was just a matter of pronunciation. Well, maybe not that simple, but less difficult than starting from scratch. Both of us developed a second voracious appetite for reading English. My brother read the entire Encyclopedia Brittanica. I read a lot of it but not all.

I've mentioned my brother's physical prowess, but he also has a brilliant intellect. On my first day in Junior High School, the same one he had just graduated from, I was in Social Studies class waiting for seat assignments. When the teacher saw my name, he asked if Carmelo was my brother. I said yes. To my astonishment, the teacher then said, "Take a seat in the back, you have an "A" for the class." I was a little embarrassed at the jeering and ribbing I got. I still did all the work required and completed all assignments. I was an A student just like my brother, but just had to try a little harder.

Back to my college days. The first CLEP test I took was Spanish 1 and Spanish 2. I aced both and earned 12 college credits. My second test was The Humanities which deals with Art, Literature, Music, and Architecture. None, except literature were among my favorite subjects. I spent several days visiting the Philadelphia Museum of Art and asked a lot of questions. I had to learn about Cubism, Abstract, Modern and many other art forms. I was familiar with Michelangelo, DaVinci, Picasso, and other masters so this was not so difficult. Music and Architecture were a bit more challenging.

I played the flute in elementary school, so I had a little knowledge of musical terms and symbols. I found some CLEP study guides and prep tests online which were a great help with subjects I might be a little weak in. The effort was successful and garnered another six credits in an hour test.

Next in line was Natural Sciences which include Astronomy, Biology, Chemistry and Geology. I do not know the difference between an igneous and sedimentary rock, but I wanted to be an Astronomer when younger and read many books on the subject. I was also well read on Biology, and a little less on Chemistry. Those three were enough to make up for my limitation in Geology. Voila! Six more credits in the books. The last test was College English Composition.

I wrote my first published story at age 12 and have been practicing since then. It would have been embarrassing to fail this one. This last test added 6 more for a total of 30 credits, which is the maximum allowed in the CLEP program. One year of college attendance eliminated with just a few tests. Earn College Credit with CLEP – CLEP | College Board https://collegeboard.org

Need to pause for a brief flash back to explain my first published work at age 12. When I was in elementary school, there was a kids' newspaper called the Weekly Reader. The paper offered a statewide writing contest. As far back as I can remember, especially recalling my exasperating ordeal dressed in the monk's habit my mother made me wear as an offering to the virgin she hoped would keep me from dying, I developed an antagonism and distaste for religious dogma and rituals, therefore I chose to write an essay about religion.

I began researching past and present religious beliefs and their effects on society. I read up on Greek and Roman Mythology, Buddhism, Islam, (back then known as Mohammedanism), Judaism and Christianity, among others. There was no internet in the fifties, so I relied on Encyclopedias and the public library. My entry in the contest was an essay comparing ancient religions with the modern ones. I concluded that since the old religions became extinct and replaced by those popular today, there was no guarantee that the new ones would last forever. I also determined that someone or a determined group had to have come up with the idea of organizing primitive beliefs into a coordinated system in order to gain control and power over the masses. I did not win but got honorable mention. My teacher said I could have won if I had not suggested that today's religions were doomed to extinction just like the old ones. The thought of stretching my childhood essay into something more elaborate simmered in my head for decades until 2017, when I believed my end was at hand and it was time to fulfill a lifelong goal. This episode in my life will continue in a few pages.

Back to my college days. I was about to complete my second year and needed to find methods that could earn more credits so I could get my Bachelor of Science degree in two years instead of four.

I found a way. There are two other programs that offer credits without attending class. They are PLA or Prior Learning Assessment and Experiential Essays.

PLA allows a student to convert (non-college) schooling or training into college credits. This was the easiest way to early graduation. All that is required is a certificate, diploma or other documentation for non-academic courses or training. I sent in proof of my military training,

Sheriff's Academy and even my SCUBA diving certificate. Only got one credit for that, but every little bit helps. I still swim almost daily so that training is still producing benefits. Years ago, neither Police Academy training nor Sheriff's Academy training earned college credits. Now both Academies earn college credits.

Experiential Essays are just that. If you have experience in a particular field (There are hundreds of categories) you can write a 1000-word essay for 1 credit, 2000 for 2 and 3000 words earn you 3 credits. I wrote three 3000-word essays in a week. I needed a total of 30 credits to skip the last year and received them by combining PLA with the Essays.

I graduated in 23 months instead of 4 years. I did hurt myself in a way, since the VA monthly education stipend ended upon graduation. Although the actual cash not received totaled close to $21,000, it was well worth it. I was getting bored taking classes on subjects I already was proficient in. In a few days, I earned more than the 30 credits I needed to eliminate the fourth year of college. These credits can be used only for electives not for the major course of study. Basically, one cannot CLEP out of Brain Surgery classes.

I never applied for a writing job again. I just continued writing articles and toying with book ideas. One of the 3000-word essays happened to be about Genealogy, and I considered stretching the essay to book length. The BS degree just gave me more legitimacy or credentials as a writer.

I started working on some book projects but always found an excuse to do something else. It was much more enjoyable to hop on a plane and visit my home island as well as other adventurous trips.

I kept busy but not doing anything of great importance. For many years, an idea for a story had been percolating in my brain. I would think of it often and add an idea or a twist to the tale. I do not know what kept me from starting to put pen to paper or later, fingers to keyboard. I probably believed that I had a lot of time left to bring the project to fruition.

On May 16, 2017, disaster struck. The massive heart attack I mentioned earlier almost did me in after flat lining twice. I survived of course, but it took me months to recover, and even then, not fully. I've already written about that ordeal except that I was in physical therapy for over several months to regain simple skills like walking or reaching for a can of soup in a cabinet. Lucky that my oldest granddaughter sacrificed her time to take care of me and my 93-year-old mother.

My prognosis was not too favorable, and I believed that another myocardial infarction would finish me for good. Since I was somewhat disabled, could not travel or even drive, I was stuck at home. I realized that the story (hinted to a few pages back) that had been percolating in my head for years needed to be set free. I could still type and had all the research facilities at my fingertips on the internet.

Since the main plot and characters, though still nameless, were almost fully developed, I wrote the book in three weeks, but needed another few months to edit, polish and revise. End result: *In the Beginning – The Early Days of Religious Beliefs* (bit.ly/jrey45)

When I believed it was finished, I sent it to my publisher and began to translate the novel into Spanish. As I worked on the translation, I watched my youngest great-granddaughter running around creating the kind of havoc only a toddler can do. I suddenly realized that my story had no prominent female characters. With the changing but positive current attitude about female rights and their true value in today's society, I needed to make a change.

I called the publisher and asked for a temporary halt on publishing while I made some changes including adding an important character. It did not take long. I named her Mina, which is close to the name of my source of inspiration.

A few thousand words later the newly imagined warrior/priestess was creating mayhem in her own Paleolithic world of long ago.

She has become the most popular character in the book, and I am considering a sequel. But this current project has priority for the moment.

As I grow older, I sometimes believe that I spend more time in the hospital than home. Diabetes has made me susceptible to foot infections and I've been admitted three times in the last year. Nothing to worry about, I recover eventually but surely without requiring critical care.

AGENT ORANGE
1965 – The end

"How people die remains in the memory of those who live on"
—Dame Cicely Saunders

The events in this chapter did not begin immediately after the end of my military obligation in fact, the inexorable consequences had already begun to fester inside me and inside thousands of unsuspecting American soldiers the minute most set foot in 'Nam.

Despite my body's reluctance to accept the end and fade to black, I am not immune to illness, nor am I totally unbreakable. Exposure to Agent Orange, a toxic herbicide used in Vietnam has taken a gradual but persistent toll on my health.

There are numerous ailments usually referred to as "presumptive diseases" by the Veterans Administration connected to the toxic herbicide. Unfortunately, due to exposure to Agent Orange in the war zone, I acquired several of those diseases while some undiagnosed others may be lurking in my cells waiting their turn to cause more havoc.

Agent Orange is one of the several types of herbicides used in 'Nam to defoliate the jungle thereby eliminating forest cover and crops needed by the enemy. American planes poured over 20 million gallons of the poisonous solution over the forests and fields of Vietnam, Laos, and Cambodia. There were various mixtures used and identified by the color of the 55-gallon drums containing Agent White, Agent Pink, Agent Blue, Agent Purple, and Agent Green. The most used and by far, the most dangerous was Agent Orange. It is estimated that more than 3.6 million acres of land were contaminated affecting over four million people, (not sure if that estimate includes the number of American soldiers who served in the war.

What I found unusual is that the real culprit is DIOXIN (TCDD) but that is not part of the recipe used directly in the manufacture of the color-coded herbicides. It is formed as a by-product during manufacture. The manufacturers are also to blame for not evaluating the side effects effectively. The nine companies involved in the production and distribution are:Dow Chemical Company,Monsanto Company,Diamond Shamrock Corporation,Hercules Inc., Thompson Hayward Chemical Co.,United States Rubber Company(Uniroyal), Thompson Chemical Co.,Hoffman-Taff Chemicals, Inc., and Agriselect. - Agent Orange - Wikipedia

However it was made, the problem was that not only did it destroy the foliage but killed the Vietnamese people and American soldiers, just not as quickly as the vegetation. The defoliation program was code named Operation Ranch Hand. What I find difficult to accept is the illogical belief that spraying an entire country with millions of gallons of poison would not affect both friend and foe. This was an extreme version of "friendly fire".

In 1988, Dr. James Clary, an Air Force researcher associated with Operation Ranch Hand, wrote to Senator Tom Daschle,

"When we initiated the herbicide program in the 1960s, we were aware of the potential for damage due to dioxin contamination in the herbicide. However, because the material was to be used on the enemy, none of us were overly concerned. We never considered a scenario in which our own personnel would become contaminated with the herbicide."- https://www.history.com/topics/vietnam-war/agent-orange-1

That doctor's conclusion has to be among the most idiotic ones ever voiced by a medical researcher and apparent military advisor. How can this alleged scientist claim that they expect the poison to affect only the enemy. The job of the military is to search for, find and then engage the enemy. To accomplish that, soldiers have to end up in the enemy's environment. The politicians he addressed are or were just as responsible, just as ignorant and just as responsible for the catastrophic effects.

As my year of duty progressed, I did not know that my internal organs were slowly absorbing contaminants that more than likely would eventually overpower my unique talent for avoiding a definitive demise.

From 1964 to 1972 over three million American soldiers served in Southeast Asia, most deployed to Vietnam. Over 58,000 names are etched on the black granite wall I mentioned earlier in memory of those who died in that conflict. More than 150,000 service men received non-mortal wounds. What is not usually discussed, or maybe even realized is that most of the millions that came home, including those that earned Purple Hearts for visible injuries, also received non discernible wounds that would smolder in their bodies only to flare up when least expected. In time, sometimes years, the "invisible wounds" would begin making their lives miserable, suffering from a variety of ailments that may not have developed if not for Agent Orange. Veterans of the most unpopular war in American history are dying slowly but likely faster than they would have if they had not received unapparent and slowly developing medical trauma caused by exposure to poison delivered by our own aircraft under orders from our own high command.

Below is a list of some of the presumptive diseases, some of which are currently challenging my survival skills. One or two have already temporarily succeeded. Diabetes Mellitus, Ischemic Heart Disease, Multiple Myeloma, Non-Hodgkin's Lymphoma, Parkinson's Disease, Peripheral Neuropathy, Early- Onset Porphyria Cutanea Tarda, Prostate Cancer, Lung cancer, Respiratory Cancers, Soft Tissue Sarcomas, Hypertension, et al. More are added on a regular basis.

There is a recently added program called the PACT ACT or Promise to Address Comprehensive Toxics (PACT) Act. I've recently been sent to a VES (Veterans Evaluation Servave show great devotion to hices) center to determine if any of the latest presumptive maladies have attacked my immune system. One concern is that most, if not all, are progressive and potentially terminal. The greatest concern is the increasing debilitating factor that accompanies these horrific maladies. In simpler terms, I become unhealthier and less functional as the months and years pass by. I do not fear death. I've looked it in the eye too many times to tremble at its approach. What I truly abhor is the possibility of living, but incapacitated, unable to care for myself and depending on others for my every need. That, I would not wish on anyone, especially me or members of my family who have displayed great devotion for my care in times of physical stress. Before I am in that helpless, needy condition, I would rather welcome a final encounter with the Angel of Death but definitely not by my own hand.

The Veterans Administration is now battling another era of non-battle ailments also caused by toxins, but this time, not Agent Orange or of any other hue. The toxins poisoning American soldiers is now created in "burn pits". A burn pit is a common military way of getting rid of waste material which may include plastics, fuel, oil, garbage, rubber and even human waste. Just about anything considered unwanted trash gets thrown in. It is usually an open-air area that can accommodate all kinds of waste in large quantities. Th airborne residue mixes with dust and other pollutants already present in Afghanistan's and Iraq's environments. The Military has closed most of the pits and expects to close them all.

It is inconceivable that the so-called experienced military experts and the assemblage of highly educated (?) medical advisers did not absorb any lessons from their imbecilic mismanagement of the catastrophic conflict that was Vietnam. Not only in tactics, strategy, objectives, and leadership, but in much simpler policies like getting rid of trash, or foliage, without jeopardizing the collective health of their entire in-country military force.

No one is sure of the exact numbers of Vietnam Veterans affected by exposure to the silent killer. A recent estimate claims over 400,000 have died. That number is almost five times the number of those killed in combat. There are currently many thousands receiving treatment for one or more of the listed diseases, including me. The death toll will definitely rise as veterans age and the severity of the conditions progress and more presumptive ailments are added to the list. The population of Vietnam suffered or are suffering still. About 4 million Vietnamese citizens have been affected. -Southeastasiaglobe.com

Most of my close friends, including lifelong ones have already passed away, all due to exposure to Agent Orange. One was more like a brother. He was born in the same bed I was born in, but a year earlier. It bothers me somewhat that I have outlived many others who were victimized by the same silent killer and even though some were exposed after I was, and some were nearly the same age or younger.

As I grow older, I sometimes believe that I spend more time in the hospital than at home. Diabetes and a poorly functioning heart has made me susceptible to foot infections and I've been admitted three times in the last year. Nothing to worry about, I recover eventually but surely without requiring critical care during those in patient situations. I believe the recent hospitalizations triggered the actions my doctors suggested to me in the following paragraph.

I was recently called to meet with a group of doctors at the VA to discuss a new program for patients like me. The first thing they did was hand me a brochure explaining something called Palliative care. Those words surprised me. I was also told that The team leader of my Palliative team is my cardiologist. I looked to him and said, "isn't that related to hospice care. "Yes", he said, "There are three levels of hospice care, level three is when you are admitted to a center that will provide comfort care and nothing else, because there is no cure for your condition. Level two is almost the same except that since the condition is less serious, the patient can receive care at home. We are offering you level one, which we determine would be most comfortable for you. You won't need home care but you can continue out-patient care, but knowing that there is little we can do to eliminate some of your conditions. You will not be cured but we can provide services that will help manage the illnesses until you need level two or three. I said, "So it is the first step in getting me ready for the inevitable." He said, "Well maybe not that drastic, you may continue at your level for years – maybe not getting better but not necessarily getting worse either.

This train of thought reminds me of a conversation I had with my father during his last days. He was 92 and knew he did not have much time left. We all knew. I asked him, "Pop, are you afraid of dying?"

He smiled and answered, "Why should I be afraid of something that happens or will happen to everyone." He smiled more broadly and almost laughed. I truly believe that he wanted to add, "Except you."

U.S. Air Force planes spray the defoliant chemical Agent Orange over dense vegetation in South Vietnam in this 1966 black-and-white file photo. Photo: AP

FOOTNOTES

In the introduction to this book, I mentioned the Lazarus Syndrome got its name because of the Biblical character raised by Jesus. When I wrote that I was reminded that I've always been puzzled by that alleged miracle. Why was he risen? The man named Lazarus did nothing of note after being resurrected. Why bring someone back who made no notable contribution to humanity? The strangest part was that he was raised 4 days after being entombed. There is a passage that states that he stunk as he walked out of his tomb. The act begs another question, Why was he raised after decomposition was already in progress? I also wonder why people who are believers don't question any of this. Even though I am not a devotee, I had to look for a possible explanation.

I found this: Using the Bible's own words John-11:4 suggests that Jesus wanted to impress his disciples by bringing someone back who had been dead for a while, not like the others who were revived relatively closer to their time of death. John-11:55 implies that Jesus also wanted to prove his power over death before he was to be crucified.

This link below deals with what happens to the physical body after it uses up all Lazarus Effect opportunities, NDE's, OBEs and any other restoration attempt. I was going to comment on the data but found it too gruesome to include in detail. It read more like an Edgar Alan Poe morbid tale. Go for it if you dare.

What happens to your body when you die - step by step - CoventryLive (coventrytelegraph.net)

Speaking of one of my favorite authors, many of his macabre stories dealt with death and dying. The plot of one was about maintaining a man alive using hypnosis, referred to as mesmerizing in that era.

The last chapter reads:

"…Finally, the narrator makes attempts to awaken Valdemar by asking questions that are answered with difficulty, as Valdemar's voice emanates from his throat and lolling tongue, but his lips and jaws are frozen in death. In between trance and wakefulness, Valdemar begs the narrator to put him back to sleep quickly or to waken him. As Valdemar shouts "Dead! Dead!" repeatedly, the narrator starts to bring him out of his trance, only for his entire body to immediately decay into a "nearly liquid mass of loathsome—of detestable putrescence." The Facts in the Case of M. Valdemar. *Edgar Alan Poe 1845*

The last few words of that paragraph are part of the disgusting steps mentioned in the text of the aforementioned link detailing "what happens to your body when you die."

Epilogue

My initial goal was to discuss the Lazarus Syndrome, NDEs and OBEs but the research sent me into information tributaries that led to other areas related to health, paralysis, deep comas, elements of trauma, birth, after life theories, religion, cryogenics, and others. Eventually I veered off to Artificial Intelligence and implanted neuron chips. There is so much information and so little time to review, absorb it and put the knowledge to good use. I hope that this book finds its way into young hands and inspires a few young readers to select one of the scientific or medical fields mentioned here. Elon Musk is advertising for needed help. He claims the new technologies will need thousands of engineers, computer experts, surgeons, and all other branches of medicine, electronics and technology.

I was surprised that my troublesome birth was not as unique as I first believed. Out of four million births per year, at least ten percent require resuscitation. That's about four hundred thousand babies every year. It wasn't until 1987 when Doctors Raghuveer and Cox took action and devised a plan to identify newborns in distress and suggested treatment methods. *Talkad s. Raghuveer, MD, and Austin J. Cox, MD - Am Fam Physician. 2011;83(8):911-918*

The fact that I was so personally affected by my own Lazarus Syndrome led me to wonder about others who experienced the same and the residual effects that followed. I found that religious beliefs play a strong part in what happens during NDEs and after reviving. Most of those directly involved and their families give more credit to miraculous acts than to medical intervention.

I have always wondered why religious people, especially the ultra-religious ones want to go to heaven, and enjoy eternal bliss, but, overall, are terrified of dying.

Speaking of so-called "eternal bliss," I fear that kind of existence more than I fear death itself. No worries, even if it does exist, I certainly am not on the invited list. The thrill of a roller coaster ride lasts just seconds. Likewise for an orgasm. Even being tickled becomes painful after a short while. If any of the thrills mentioned lasted much longer, they would cease to be thrilling and may likely become agonizing. Eternal paradise may also become boring after never-ending days of sunshine and gentle breezes. Or worse, sitting on a cloud, playing a harp, and ceaselessly worshipping a deity who craves attention. Another factor is that a day on the beach enjoying surf and sand is enjoyable but more so when compared to stormy days or trapped in a car or home due to blizzards in the cold of winter. I prefer the variety of changing seasons and sometimes challenging weather. Sorry, the thought of permanent celestial euphoria appears more hellish than heavenly.

I've consulted with many doctors including NIH longevity researchers, VA Hospital Specialists and Medicare Primary Care physicians and the specialists I get referred to. Only a few are familiar with the Lazarus Phenomenon, although I suspect that some of those were reluctant to admit personal involvement in any cases.

Those that were willing to address the issue provided valuable information and made an effort to diagnose or opinionate on some of my frequent revivifications. None, however made any effort to formulate an impression or speculate on my many "close calls" which were not really Lazarus events since none resulted in cardiac arrest although some of them caused my BP to crash to very dangerous levels but not quite enough to stop my heart or cause permanent damage. I will still continue to wonder what made me nervous, strongly enough to stop my car on that night on I-95. I will consider any suggestions.

There are a few factors that offer me some protection. One is genetics. My diverse genetic ancestry, especially my long-lived parents, provided a very effective immune system. Both parents survived into their 90's and both easily and successfully battled cancer, strokes, and heart problems. And most gratifying, not a hint of dementia.

Another clue to my durability may be my seemingly unbreakable bones. During my first visit to John's Hopkins Longevity Study, the technician congratulated me on my thick bones after a whole-body bone scan. The tech said that I had the bones of an 18-year-old. I've never had a seriously broken bone. Just two insignificant cracks to an ankle and wrist. Writing this section, just recalled 10 feet fall from a ladder unto a concrete wall edge; it certainly hurt like hell but needed no medical care. This was one of my many "close calls." I cannot fully credit genealogy nor a well-functioning immune system for avoiding death or even serious injury. Since I don't believe in supernatural beings such as guardian angels, ethereal protectors, invisible superhero, or finally, divine intervention I can only call it pure dumb luck.

Whatever it may be, I will exploit it for as long as possible, well aware that like my father said, sooner or later, everybody dies. Including me.

THE END (?)

Sources

Page 7: https://my.clevelandclinic.org/health/symptoms/22920-asystole

Page 7: https://www.ems1.com/medical-treatment/articles/rosc-after-death-the-lazarus-syndrome-WfDfxqI9As8diGUq/ -Marianne Myers BS 8/31/2020

Page 7: *Gordon L, Pasquier M, Brugger H and Paal P. Autoresuscitation (Lazarus phenomenon) after termination of cardiopulmonary resuscitation – a scoping review. Scandinavian Journal of Trauma, Resuscitation and Emergency Medicine, 2020. 28(14).*

Page 16: *A Life From Beginning to End copyright 2020 by Hourly History.* https://www.pablopicasso.org/picasso-facts.jsp

Page 16*: Saved By the Cigar by Jack Bettridge*

https://www.cigaraficionado.com/article/saved-by-the-cigar-242

https://www.historyvshollywood.com/reelfaces/breakthrough/

https://www.imdb.com/title/tt7083526/plotsummary/

https://www.youtube.com/watch?v=BGwxAitvJT8

https://www.youtube.com/watch?v=uT0DaoZyf3I

https://www.youtube.com/results?search_query=justin+smith+frozen+man

https://www.youtube.com/watch?v=XIV7TJwI-_s

https://www.youtube.com/watch?v=CK1lude7gjM

Page 22: https://www.historyvshollywood.com/reelfaces/breakthrough/

Page 22: https://www.imdb.com/title/tt7083526/plotsummary/

Page 23: Talkad s. Raghuveer, MD, and Austin J. Cox, MD - *Am Fam Physician.* 2011;83(8):911-918

Page 23: https://historycollection.com/author/alexa/

Page 23: "The Lazarus phenomenon is a grossly underreported event," notes Maxillofacial Surgeon Dr. Vaibhav Sahni *Sage Journals 2016*

Page 24: https://www.healthline.com/health/lazarus-syndrome

Page 24: Patrick J. Oneill Phd. MD. FACS of Arizona Trauma and Acute Care Consortium (AZTRACC) on a YouTube video details various facts of the "rare but real"

Page 24: Talkad s. Raghuveer, MD, and Austin J. Cox, MD - *Am Fam Physician.* 2011;83(8):911-918

Page 25: Dr. Vaibhav Sahni *Sage Journals 2016*

"The Eternal Promise".The Verge. 2015.Archived*from the original on 2023-03-25:. Retrieved2021-01-22.*

Page 25: "The Lazarus phenomenon is a grossly underreported event," notes Maxillofacial Surgeon Dr. Vaibhav Sahni *Sage Journals 2016*

https Page 25: The Countess' Path://historycollection.com/author/alexa/

Page 26: Frozen Bodies Brought Back to Life? Cryogenics and the Science of Immortality | Documentary - YouTube

Cryonics - Wikipedia

Page 28: *Science - Adam Hoffman March 31, 2016*

Page 29: Adhiyaman V, Adhiyaman S and Sundaram R. The Lazarus phenomenon. Journal of the Royal Society of Medicine, 2007. 100(12): 552-557.

Page 29: What does CPR have to do with the curious case of clinically dead patients coming "back to life"? Adam Hoffman March 31, 2016

Page 31: *Cleveland Clinic, Ohio - My Cleveland Clinic.org*

Page 31: *Between Life and Death: Terri Schiavo's Story Peacock, MSNBC Dec 3, 2023*

Page 31 Patrick J. Oneill Phd. MD. FACS of Arizona Trauma and Acute Care Consortium (AZTRACC) on a YouTube

Page 32: The Lazarus phenomenon: When the 'dead' come back to life (medicalnewstoday.com)

Page 34: Comatose Cases

Page 35: Came Back Wrong - What's Going On With The Lazarus Pit? Andrew Henderson Jun 1, 2022

Page 35: https://en.wikipedia.org/wiki/File:Wiertz_burial.jpg This work is in the public domain in the United States because it was published (or registered with the <u>U.S. Copyright Office</u>) before January 1, 1928.

Page 36: More Cases

Page 38: *The Daily Mail.com 2014* <u>Kate Allatt – Don't lower your expectations!</u>

Page 39: en.wikipedia.org/wiki/Tardigrade

Page 40: <u>Fear of Being Buried Alive Phobia - Taphophobia | FEAROF</u>

Page 45: Close Calls

Page 47: John F. Kennedy Inaugural Speech January 1961

Page 50: <u>John B. Gordon - Wikipedia</u>

Page 53: Military Service

Page 61: Vietnam

Page 63: Viet Cong attack on Tan Son Nhut Air Base (1966)

<u>Viet Cong attack on Tan Son Nhut Air Base (1966) | Military Wiki | Fandom</u>

Page 65: <u>https://www.history.com/topics/vietnam-war/agent-orange-1</u>

Page 66: <u>https://www.history.com/topics/vietnam-war/agent-orange-1</u>

Page 74: *Southeastasiaglobe.com*

Page 80: <u>Earn College Credit with CLEP – CLEP | College Board</u>

Page 83: *(1) National Geographic, The Story of God with Morgan Freeman. S1 Ep1 – Beyond Death*

Page 84: *Huda. "Islam on the Afterlife." Learn Religions, Aug. 26, 2020, learnreligions.com/islam-on-the-afterlife-2004337.*

Page 86: *Dr Sam Pernia, (2014-11-01) death and Consciousness-an overview of the mental and cognitive experience of death.*

Page 86:   Life After Life: The Bestselling Original Investigation That Revealed "Near-Death Experiences"*Raymond Moody MD 1975* <u>www.lifefterlife.com</u>

Page 87: *Life After Life: The Bestselling Original Investigation That Revealed "Near-Death Experiences"Raymond Moody MD 1975*

Page 88: *Life After Life: The Bestselling Original Investigation That Revealed "Near-Death Experiences"Raymond Moody MD 1975*

Page 90: *ChatAI.com 2023*

Page 91: *AI at AWS 2023*Page 94: Series C Funding Round Announcement | Blog | NeuralinkPage 96: *Elon Musk Neuralink Presentation YouTube*

Page 96: 10 Amazing Things Scientists Just Did withCRISPR

www.livescience.com/59602-crispr-advances-gene-editing-field.html

Page 99: *Talkad s. Raghuveer, MD, and Austin J. Cox, MD – Am Fam Physician. 2011;83(8):911–918*

Kuisma M, Salo A, Puolakka J, et al. Delayed return of spontaneous circulation (the Lazarus phenomenon) after cessation of out-of-hospital cardiopulmonary resuscitation. Resuscitation, 2017. 118: 107-111.

Also by Jaime Reyes:

How did primitive beliefs develop and evolve into the most powerful persuasive force ever developed?

In the Beginning: The Early Days of Religious Beliefs is a riveting read regarding the origin, development, and conceptualization of religious bodies as perceived through the wide lens of Author Jaime Reyes' keen eye and sharp judgment. Reyes looks to unravel an old saying that suggested the genesis of belief ideologies and practices to have had its root in avaricious individuals who greedily strived to gain control over gullible and unsuspecting populaces.

The storyline revolves around a self-proclaimed priest, Og, who has discovered the prodigious returns he can gather after manipulating the village chief and his subjects with a highly deceptive spiritual performance in their most troublesome moment. He claims to possess a rare gift that gives him the means to communicate with the spirits presumably responsible for dreadful storms such as the one currently looming over his village. Unaware, the deeply apprehensive inhabitants can't help but cling to the elderly cave-dweller's wisdom and spiritual prowess which promises hope for survival against the gods' destructive rage. Og's artifice would later see him bestowed with singular honor and admiration as his status and influence substantially shifted from the biting threat of obscurity and misery to a glorified seat at the Chief's high table.

Reyes' imagination in this fictional work will have readers amused by the levels of susceptibility characters who lack strong critical thinking may find themselves fading into. As has been plotted out in the text, today's society is equally wrapped up in similar snares where desperate individuals have found themselves entangled in deceptive spiritual circles through shrewd figures who disguised themselves as promoters of peace and as spiritual guides, without careful consideration of their origin and doctrine. I find the author's sentiments adaptable considering his deep research that brings awareness to the naturalness of falling for the protagonist's charismatic and charming nature in employing hoaxes and seduction to lure people.

In the Beginning: The Early Days of Religious Beliefs is conclusively a must-read text that will not only challenge its readers' belief system but also compel more vigilance against persons and sects who claim to offer safety and healing for emotionally vulnerable people. Reyes' elating publication can be read in one sitting and will have you informed, satisfied, and longing for another of his thought-provoking reads. Highly recommend!
—*Pacific Book Review*